# THE SHAADI BROUHAHA..

# THE SHAADI BROUHAHA..

*arranged marriage hungama*

Anjlee Shah

Srishti
PUBLISHERS & DISTRIBUTORS

**Srishti Publishers & Distributors**
N-16, C. R. Park
New Delhi 110 019
editorial@srishtipublishers.com

First published by
Srishti Publishers & Distributors in 2015



10 9 8 7 6 5 4 3 2 1

All characters in this book are fictitious, and any resemblance to real persons, living or dead, is purely coincidental. The mention of social networking sites and matchmaking websites is only with reference to the story and the author does not intent to comment/criticize/defame anyone in the process.



Printed and bound in India

*For Pappa,*
*You did not live forever,*
*However, my love for you shall…*

# Acknowledgements

They say that you are lucky if you have someone in your life who has more trust in you than you have in yourself. That way, I am the most fortunate person because I have a team of such exceptional people who have supported me throughout this journey. I would like to say thanks to:

- First and foremost, my parents, for bringing me into this world and giving me unconditional love and support.
- Binita, my sister, a part of my heart. Without her constant encouragement, this book would have never been written.
- My loving husband Ritesh, for standing by my side and being understanding on weekends while I was writing this book.
- Vishal, my brother-in-law, one of the most humble human beings and a consistent supporter of my work.
- My grandmother, for her extremely positive attitude towards life and unwavering faith in me.
- Bhavini, my best friend, for her immensely calm demeanour and continuous motivation throughout this project.
- Pooja and Chitra, my truest friends for being with me through different times.
- The entire team at Srishti, for seeing the potential in my manuscript and giving me the opportunity to convert it into a book.

- Sunill Kaushik and Inkstudioz for designing an amazing cover for this book.
- Lastly, a huge shout-out of thanks to all the readers who picked up this book and put their trust in a debut author!

I will look forward to your feedback on the book. You can reach me at, www.facebook.com/theshaadibrouhaha or connect on Twitter at @shahanjlee.

# Dollarkumar

'Launching a newbie into the matrimonial market *na*, is like launching a new iPhone in a saturated market. You have to be sleek, thin and better than the previous versions. Unless your product has distinctive advantages, it won't sell. You have to enhance the strengths and hide the weaknesses if you want public interest and yes, low-maintenance is a must ... irrespective of the gender,' marketing guru Monali bhabhi enhanced the salient features of a desired matrimonial partner. My mother had suggested that it would be a good idea for her to help me fill out the shaadi.com profile.

'Sleek?! Please. I am a well-figured girl. I just have five–six kilos to lose and besides, I read an article in a men's magazine, where a survey proved that curvaceous women are preferred,' I defended myself.

'*Achha*? And who was featured on the cover page?' bhabhi asked stretching her arms over her head.

'A size hero Heidi Klum in a two-piece bikini,' I said, sadly. She gave a victorious smile.

I silently wrote fifty-five kilos, three kgs short of my actual weight.

'Fine! Got your point. But what is this all about being low-maintenance. I mean, come on! If a guy wants her partner to look like a Victoria's Secret model, she can't be low maintenance. There is a whole team of trainers, nutritionists, make-up artists and plastic surgeons working on her, who charge a bomb for their services ... it's their profession to look good.' I wasn't the one to give up so easily.

'Fair point.' Bhabhi nodded.

'Profession CA... Company Axis Bank...' I kept typing the information.

'Next question is pretty straightforward. Age. Twenty-five...' I punched in the numbers.

'Tch tch.' Monali bhabhi shook her head. 'Grave mistake. You should have started looking for guys much before. Apparently the girls who are recent graduates, about the age of twenty-one or twenty-two, are more desirable. Chances for you are not as good as that age group, but then, not as bad as thirty also,' she said.

'Okay, beat this. Once Pappu uncle asked me to meet a guy for matrimony when I was nineteen, just nineteen,' I said rolling my eyes.

'You are joking, right?' Bhabhi said unbelievingly.

'That's what I told him. He tried to convince me *ke beta* you're an adult now *na? Ladka toh dekh lo*, settle down later after graduation,' I said shaking my head in disbelief.

'Hmm... but make sure that you land up with a guy in a year, maximum. Look at our Falgun bhai. He is thirty-two, single and lonely. Poor guy, he rarely attends any family function. The boat has sailed in his case,' sighed Monali bhabhi.

'I think it has more to do with relatives and friends around him who keep pestering him with annoying matrimonial questions. In fact, I find him quite cool. He writes wonderful columns for *Gujarat Samachar*.' I said, shuffling the pen between my thumb and index finger. *God, why can't I sit still!*

She took the pen from my hand and tapped it on my forehead. 'Yes, but all those columns don't fill the void of a partner, understood?'

Was she right? Having a partner in your life...is it that important? Why can't one get married to causes, careers or goals and ... be happy?

'Next question.' She snapped her fingers.

'Caste. Brahmin,' I said aloud, 'and preferred partner is any Gujarati-speaking *chhokro*.'

'Hema *Foi* okay with this?' questioned bhabhi.

'Very much,' I responded.

'*Manglik dosh,*' I said reading out the options. 'Yes, no or don't know?'

'This one, I know.' Monali bhabhi added, 'Ninety-nine percent of the lot who write don't know are *manglik*. Of course they cannot put it out just like that to face rejection even before someone gets past their basic profile. What about you? Are you *manglik*?' she asked twitching her eyebrows?

'Maybe,' I winked, as I moved towards the 'Hobbies and Interests' column.

SHE THUMPED TWO fullscapes and three photo albums on the coffee table in front of us. The fullscapes had names, addresses, telephone numbers and qualifications of prospective grooms and the photo albums had two pictures each – one close-up face shot and the other standing.

The poses were patterned. Either they had their fists under the chin for support or they rested one foot uncomfortably over a chair with one hand on the thigh and another at the waist. Their names and numbers were written behind each photo for easy identification.

Matchmaker Nilam ben looked at her treasure and smiled. She rose to fame in the late nineties when she turned her favourite pastime, matchmaking, into a serious business. Before long she became the 'saviour' of innumerable parents and their off-springs of marriageable age. Every parent thanked god for Nilam ben, for without her, they'd be doomed.

'This is my *baby* Nitya, CA pass without fail (she meant in the first attempt) and currently working with Axis Bank,' mom introduced me. Whether you are fourteen or forty, if you are a Gujju child, your parents will introduce you as their *babo* or *baby*.

'Go no, touch her feet,' she nudged with such excitement that I fell straight at Nilam ben's feet.

'*Jeeti re, jeeti re.*' Godmother placed her divine hand on my head. 'Hmmm... look-wise *toh* your daughter is like Saira Banu... very beautiful... fair skin, brown eyes, brown hair, *bas* her height is little less.' She examined me from head to toe as if casting me for a role in a daily soap. 'What's your height baby?' she questioned.

'Five-two or five-three? What should I say?' my mom always asked me for an approval each time she lied.

'Baby's height is five feet one inch, aunty.' I spoke the truth. Come on, anyone can tell the difference between a couple of inches. Besides, weight is a variable measurement so you can lie on that, but height remains the same.

'No problem. Just wear high heels when you go to meet the guy.' Nilam ben suggested a 'ground-breaking' idea.

*Maybe I will just walk on my toes if I was asked to remove my shoes outside their home.* I chuckled at the thought.

'Have you brought your photographs?' she inquired.

'Exactly like you told. One half close-up photo and one standing photo.' My mom handed her the envelope with my snaps.

'What is this? No studio photo?' she looked disappointed as she examined the pictures.

'I told her a thousand times to get studio photos. But no. She wants to print photos only from the website where you can look at everyone's photo. Facelook!' Mom gave me a told-you-so look.

'Facebook,' I corrected her. She glared at me.

'The match you showed for our Sumit – Monali – is such a wonderful girl, I tell you. She has mixed with our family so well. My Nitya *toh* just loves her.' My mom did what she is good at, flattering. Nilam ben did match for many cousins of mine. My paternal uncle's son, Sumit's match was fixed by her.

'Which Sumit?' she pretended to forget or maybe she had matched so many Sumits with Monalis that she couldn't tell which one.

'My husband's elder brother Girishbhai's son,' my mom reminded her, 'the one who has travel business in Singapore.'

She said, 'Oh yeah yeah, Girish and Sons Travels. I fixed it in one meeting, Hema ben, first meeting.' She seemed to easily remember the matches if you introduce them by business.

My mom widened her eyes in appreciation and looked at me. I widened my eyes too in response. I didn't know what else to do.

'Nilam ben, show only good boys for my Nitya,' mom requested.

'Arey Hema ben, your daughter is like my daughter. She has no father and no brother, so it's my moral responsibility. And after all, I have answers to give to Him,' she pointed towards the ceiling. There were only cobwebs.

*If I am like her daughter, then will she waive off the hefty matrimonial fees?* I wondered.

'Here, fill this form!' She handed me an A4-size paper filled with usual questions – name, age, caste, education, occupation, income bracket, parents' details, email address, etc.

While I was busy filling the details, my mom noted information on the guys we were supposed to meet.

'Sahil Parekh…B E Mechanical…26 years…
Baroda…9876543323.'

'Abhay Maniar...IT Engineer...29 years
Pune...7897897899.'

Nilam ben dictated at a lightning speed; it was getting hard for mom to keep up.

'Dollarkumar Purohit...MBA...27 years...California... 7868768989...coming to India this December. He is very handsome, *dekhte reh jaoge.* Wait I will show his photo.' She leaned over to fetch his snap from the album.

Indeed this Dollarkumar dude looked very cute, just like the guy next door. He had a cleft on his chin and his hair were gelled back to form neat spikes.

'Wow,' I said.

'What?' Mom and Nilam ben looked at me, confused.

'Now.' I quickly modified. 'I think we should leave now.'

Just then the door-bell rang and a guy accompanying two adults came and sat opposite us. From what it seemed, even they were here for their son's matrimony.

'This is Ayush Patel...B.Com LLB, perfect for your daughter. They just bought a new three BHK flat in Nanpura. Wonderful family Hema ben, wonderful.' She introduced us. I understood her tactics of using a word twice in a sentence for the emphasizing effect.

All of us were stunned and embarrassed by her words. For her, it might be common to acquaint people like this and speed up matters but it was a first for me.

'Don't think Hema ben, just jump. I am giving this boy's guarantee.' She patted her chest for visual special effects.

The bloke and his parents sitting there seemed to be delighted. They were approved by Nilam ben. My mom gave them a very hesitant smile. We thanked Nilam ben and left.

'NEXT ONE, DOLLARKUMAR from the US,' Malvika went into a fit of laughter when she read the name aloud. She sat beside me ticking off names from the list. I sent them email one by one through saved drafts enclosing my matrimonial biodata and a couple of recent pictures.

*Maybe I should link my Facebook and Twitter accounts also.*

'And what will you be called after the wedding? Poundkumari from London?' Manav gave her a quick high-five and went back to playing 'Call of Duty'.

'And their babies Oanda exchange rate,' Komal butted in and everyone split into an ear-deafening laughter.

'Ha ha ha. Very funny.' I made a face. 'Okay now listen, I have typed an email requesting his details. What should I write in signature: yours sincerely or best regards?'

'Requesting? Oh please. Why don't you just write "your most humble servant",' Manav retorted. I threw a cushion at him. He caught it like a cricket ball.

Manav-Malvika-Komal-Nitya, in one breath...that's how we were called. Everyone took our names together, in one breath, not one but couple of breaths, during our B.Com days. People usually connect when they like the same things, but Malvika, Komal and I clicked instantly because we hated the same things and the same people.

Manav is Malvika's twin and our *kachori* sponsor. He made a reputation for being the dumbest student after he failed on a leaked exam paper. He was also this close to getting kicked out from our group when he started hitting on Komal, but soon we made him our 'Rakhee' brother. I can never forget that day.

'My laptop will take at least a couple of days to get formatted,' I pondered loudly as I registered on shaadi.com, bharatmatrimony.com and every possible Indian matrimony site I could get my hands on. 'I will come here again tomorrow to check if anyone has replied at all,' I said browsing away.

'Ten rupees an hour,' said Manav as he yawned and tossed his controller on one side of the sofa. 'By the way, why do you need formatting? Too much porn isn't good for you.' He gave a devilish grin.

Picking up a six-kilogram hand-weight he started to curl his bicep through his blue superman t-shirt. Get this straight – no matter how much a boy grows up, his love for superheroes never dies.

'What rupees? Charge dollars!' Malvika gave her special suggestion as she folded the list to keep in my handbag.

I ignored them and kept browsing through the profiles on the online matrimonial portal, expressing interest in all the photogenic faces. That's how I inaugurated my account in the matrimonial market.

Different emails poured into my yahoo account as I scanned them on my smartphone one-by-one. Three spam emails told me that I had won a million dollars but had to pay a small fee to collect it; three emails from astrologers, who were ready to reveal my bright future for some cash; a Facebook profile pic-worthy picture of mine forwarded by Manav, taken on his birthday; a starred email notifying that my salary was credited. Alas, no answer from Dollarkumar.

'BUT MOM, I haven't received any reply from Dollarkumar yet. How can we just go to the airport to receive him?' I bickered, reclining the chair of the Karnavati Express.

'You keep quiet. What do you want? Someone else to turn up with their daughter before us? You know how fast these NRIs get picked up from the market? Even Nilam ben has given a green signal.' My mom retorted.

'That's her job. She can get very persuasive. Didn't you see that day?' I was furious.

'I am not going to let even a single guy slip out of our hand. That's it.' She turned her face away and started looking out of the window.

Jaina maasi received us at the Borivali station. She is my mom's third cousin, has four children and always over-powders her face. The oldest, Pinky, is about my age and rest three are boys, primary students.

'Jaina...it's good that you are in Mumbai. Where would we have gone otherwise?' my mom said with a worried expression. She looked like a lost child in a theme park.

Any relative having a home in a city, close to the international airport is, by default, host to a number of guests and also a deliveryman for general transfer of parcels.

'Don't worry Hema. Just pray that that NRI selects our Nitya and her future is secured. These US people *na* don't get home cooked food to eat. Half the deal will be closed when we will tempt him into eating delicious Indian food. He can't say no then.' Jaina maasi hatched a clever plan.

Bipin maasaji dropped us near the arrival gate and left to park his six-seater Honda. There were eight of us at the airport to receive this Dollarkumar and terrify him into submission.

Our group waited at the arrival gate. NRIs, specially the people from the US, were easily identifiable even without their luggage tag. They were fat, had a double-chin, wore XXL jeans and showed early or late signs of balding.

I saw three-four men wearing a safari suit come out of the arrival gate. A celebrity was expected.

'Oh my god! Salman Khan....' I yelled like I had hit jackpot only to realize that I was the only one shouting. Others around me were silent and looked at me as if I had lost my mind. Why

Mumbaikars don't go all hysterical when they see a celeb is beyond me. But who cares? For I saw Salman Khan, I had never seen even a Makodi Pehelwan in my life. By the time I took out my mobile to click his picture, he left sprinting faster than Usain Bolt.

'His flight is one hour late,' informed Bipin maasa. We threw bored glances at each other.

'Didi let's go and eat something,' Laalo said. Yes, food was the solution to everything – from breakups, to waiting, to plain boredom.

We girls went to a fruit stall with strings of oranges hanging on it, the kids went to a stall with packets of chips hanging all over the counter and our respective moms opened *dabbas* full of *theplas*.

'Cool na. You will be going to America. Clean roads, no pollution, no stray animals on street. Better lifestyle,' Pinky commented as she sipped her sugar-free, fresh orange juice.

'Yeah if I like the guy, and cleaner country doesn't necessarily mean better lifestyle,' I replied.

'What is for you to not like about him? He is an MBA, has a nice salary package, look wise *ekdum hero*... and *aur toh aur* he is from a foreign country.' She asked, clearly indicating that she had mugged up his biodata already. She sounds like my mom at times.

'How can you start liking someone without even meeting or talking?' I queried.

'But he is from the US.' She explained giving a very significant reason. My sixth sense could sniff her interest in Mr America already.

I kept quiet. I was thinking about my first impressions, the ones I will leave on him.

One-and-a-half hour later, I saw Dollarkumar with two wheeled trolley bags and one cabin bag slung around his shoulder. He wore a white Hollister t-shirt with baggy jeans and tousled hair. He was better-looking than his photograph.

My family exchanged happy glances. Pinky and I were happy because he was neither fat nor had a receding hairline.

I went towards him and asked 'Dollarkumar?'

'Yes?' he said with a heavy American accent.

'Hi, I am Nitya. Our parents talked about our matrimony over phone.' I extended my hand. It was most uncomfortable to be introducing myself. *What else could I have said?*

'Oh yeah. Hi! Umm... I was expecting my cousin to pick me up. Have you come with him?' He asked, visibly awkward but still handsome.

'Actually there was a slight change in plan after you boarded your flight. Our folks talked and decided that it would be the best if we hijack you first and then take you to your cousin's.' I made a bad joke.

'Oh... Ok,' he said, perplexed.

I escorted him towards the 'mob' and you could see they were 'so good' to him that he could have married me then and there, out of embarrassment.

We managed to reach Jaina maasi's home by 2 pm. It was a small house but impeccably designed. People staying in metropolitan cities sure know how to bring out the best, even in a tiny space.

'Beta, here is the bathroom, if you want to freshen up.' Jaina maasi showed him the door.

Few minutes later, we all sat cross-legged on the floor for lunch. Standard Gujarati thali was the menu. Mom and maasi fed him like there was no tomorrow.

After he downed about sixteen *puris* (I kept a mental count) my mom asked him, all concerned, 'Beta, you are not having enough. What happened? You didn't like the food?'

'*Arey* no no aunty, I have overeaten,' he said itching to loosen a couple of buttons of the denim he wore.

'Ok ok, I won't force you. Have some rice. See Jaina maasi has prepared both *daal* and *kadhi*,' said mom, dumping a ladle full of rice in his plate. He was being fed like a sacrificial goat. He couldn't reject me now. He had eaten our salt and puri after all. It was a good plan. He surveyed around to look for some help.

'Laalo, why don't show the "Dhoom Machale" step to uncle?' Bipin maasaji asked one of his boys to provide entertainment with the meal. And for Dollarkumar, I don't know which was worse – to see Laalo's dance moves or to be called an uncle.

Laalo wore his sunglasses (to get into the mood) in their living room and grooved to the tune of *Dhoom Machale*. He did a floor step sweeping his legs alternately.

'Why don't Nitya and Pinky show him the Juhu beach?' Jaina maasi suggested sightseeing after Laalo's performance.

WE SAT ON the sand as the sun set on the horizon.

'I know this is very awkward for you. I really apologize for having a meeting with you, all unannounced,' I said.

'That's ok. I know how persuasive parents are,' he said shrugging off an ant from his t-shirt with his manicured nails.

Pinky opened her shoulder-length hair and ran her hand through them. *Interesting!*

'So how often do you come to India?' I asked.

'Once in four or five years. But I take a vacation or two every year somewhere in Europe,' he showed-off.

I could hear Pinky gasp.

'What's up with your name? Dollarkumar?' I asked.

'Very embarrassing, I know. Actually my dad got a chance to go the US for the first time on the day I was born. So to keep the memory alive, he named me Dollarkumar,' he replied.

While I was trying to digest this, he hastily added, 'See listen, before we take this matter further, I want to make one thing clear.'

'What?' *My heart sank.. Here comes the girlfriend story.*

'Hmm ok... How do I put it? I am not a woman's man. I am a man's man,' he said with a discomfort in his tone.

Pinky and I looked at each other, confused.

'I am gay. I have a boyfriend back home.' There, he said it, hesitantly.

My eyes widened a little with the shock.

'Gay?' Pinky chuckled a little. 'So that means it's for real. Gay people exist and not only in the movies. I don't believe this. I am sitting in front of a gay guy. Wow,' she laughed. She tied her hair back and slumped.

Dollarkumar looked awkward.

'You do yoga. Like this.' Pinky breathed in and out rapidly through her nose. 'It will be cured.'

'Pinky!' I scolded her in a hushed tone. 'So why are you meeting girls for matrimony? Do your parents know?' I quizzed him.

'Well... sort of. They have an idea and that is why they want me to get married. I am looking for some girl who marries me and comes to the US. She lives her life and lets me live mine,' he explained.

Pinky was still dazed and the revelation had not completely sunk in yet.

'Then maybe I am not the girl for you. Somewhere down the line, I am looking for an opportunity to convert friendship into love.' I rested my case.

'Yeah I was expecting this. Could you please reject me? Tell them anything except that I am gay,' he pleaded.

'They won't understand what's gay. And I don't see any other reason to reject you. Why don't you reject me,' I suggested.

ON OUR WAY back home, Pinky was more silent than usual. Dollarkumar thanked everyone and left with his cousin in the evening.

'So did you like him or not?' Jaina maasi asked.

'Of course, yes. He is too good for me though,' I lied.

A flood of happiness ran across the room. I felt so guilty.

'I think, it will be just like Sumit and Monali. It will be finalised in the very first…' my mother began reminiscing.

'Nitya, I want to talk to you.' Pinky pulled me to a corner.

'Hey listen, you are not going to marry this guy, are you?' she asked me.

'No way.' I shook my head, 'Why?'

'Can I marry him then?'

'What?' I gave out a mini-scream.

'Shhh … don't freak out.' Pinky placed her finger to her lips.

'Pinks, he is gay. Do you even know what that means? There are more things to life than clean roads and clean environment,' I said in disbelief.

'I know. But I really want to go the US. I will be all set there. See I am not as good-looking as you, nor am I that educated. There are very less chances of me getting a guy like him. Please, understand,' she said choking on her voice.

I saw her and then I saw her buck teeth. I felt pity for her and her belief that it was the best she could do.

'But Pinks, this is not the solution.' I tried to reason with her.

'You don't understand, do you? Because you are pretty and a Chartered Accountant, you can get anyone. I am not that fortunate. I will be happy there. I know it,' she argued.

'Promise me that you will speak to maasa and maasi about it,' I murmured.

'Please don't tell them. I will speak to them in time and to Dollarkumar also,' she said, visibly relieved.

'Ok.'

'Thank you, thank you so much.' She hugged me.

'And why is he gay? It should be something in the water there,' she wondered loudly.

'HMM…AHAN…I SEE. I always knew that they are cunning people. It was entirely my fault. I shouldn't have let that Pinky go with them,' my mom was speaking to someone over the phone. I turned down the volume and began listening intently.

'What happened?' I asked my upset mom after she slammed the phone down.

'Your Pappu uncle called to give the news that their Pinky is engaged to Dollarkumar.' Pappu uncle was my mom's second cousin. He was the self-acclaimed decision-maker of our family after my father passed away.

'Our Pinky' became 'their Pinky'. Boy, mom was really angry.

'So that's great news, no?' I said casually.

'Great?' She raised her voice. 'I found the boy. I ran to Nilam ben. We spent the money to go to Mumbai. And that wretched woman comes from nowhere and steals the boy from under our nose. Shameless people! They don't even have the decency to call,' she banged some vessels into the kitchen sink.

Banging vessels is a dangerous sign. It means vacate the kitchen immediately. Even better, just get out of the house for a few hours. I can only imagine why Jaina maasi did not call.

'Everyone takes advantage of my innocence. But now you see, I will find a better boy for you than her,' spoke mom with a vengeance.

'I WOULD RATHER enter the Kurukshetra battlefield than entering the office on a Monday morning,' I said making a face as Pooja and I stood near the coffee machine for our daily dose of gossip. Pooja was the main source of our office information, gossip, politics and everything in between. She always had some juicy tid-bits to share (which she did not hesitate to make a scandal of) every single day. I loved the gossip because that was the only time she didn't gossip about me. Attention-seeker that she was, she enjoyed breaking a scoop to everyone.

'Want to hear something that will make your day?' Pooja twitched her eyebrows with an evil grin.

'What, what? Tell me quickly,' I asked as my excitement and the twinkle in my eyes rose giving her a half-lip smile. I have to admit that sometimes it's the gossip and coffee that helps one through a long office day.

'Today our new branch manager Rudra Desai is going to visit our branch for inspection. He will join from next week,' she said.

'Oh God!' I said all panicky, nearly spilling the hot coffee all over Pooja. 'I have like two files to complete from Thursday. Shit yaar and you say that this will make my day?'

'No ya. Listen to the whole thing,' she paused to take a sip of water, to build tension and also to palpate Ajay, another colleague, who was within earshot. 'A little birdie has told me that he looks absolutely breathtakingly handsome.'

'So? Even if he is George Clooney's Indian brother, I don't care. I have to finish my files. Now if you will excuse me,' I said running and dripping coffee all over the way to my desk.

'Chillax...Why are you always stuck up? Who checks files on the first day? It will just be a formal introduction...take it easy.' I heard her say behind me.

'I NEED LALBHAI Construction files,' Rudra Desai, our future branch manager said, peeping his eyes from one of the other files. He was about five feet eight or nine, with a flawless camel-coloured skin tone, high cheek bones and extra-ordinary features like a model that were to die for. George Clooney was such an understatement.

I jumped forward with the incomplete Lalbhai file and opened and shut my mouth refraining to give an explanation. I hated myself for choosing to wear glasses over contacts today. When I looked around, I could see everyone staring at him, everyone. Pooja and Jhanvi tried to catch a glimpse of his face through his file while the guys tried to figure out what brand of shoes, shirt and watch adorned this Greek god.

'You,' he said, his deep eyes penetrating mine. 'Are you responsible for Lalbhai accounts?'

'Yes sir,' I said meekly looking at him through my spectacles. I was trying my best to focus at his questions. *How can he be the branch manager? He looks so young, barely twenty-seven or twenty-eight.*

'Why is this file incomplete?' He tilted his head to one side, still pinning me down with his gaze. I was staring at him. Malvika says that staring into one's eyes for more than eight seconds will make one fall in love with that person, but in my case, it was just getting awkward.

'Sir, I was... erm... I was preoccupied planning personal income tax for M K Shah and sons,' I replied, praying to all the Gods that he wouldn't ask for the file.

'Get me M K Shah.' He summoned.

I fumbled through my drawers and handed him M K Shah. When I looked at Pooja, she shook her head. *I was oh, so dead.*

'What's your name?' He asked in a tone deeper than the Bay of Bengal.

'Nitya Trivedi.' I made a fake attempt to be confident.

'Nitya Trivedi,' he repeated. My name sounded so sexy when he spoke but I was unprepared for what followed.

'Care to explain why this,' he shook the file in the air dramatically, 'is also incomplete?'

'Sir, I was on a leave of absence on Friday, sir,' I fumbled.

'Why? Did you slip on a banana peel and injure your little head somewhere?'

I stood aghast. Such brutal words from such a lovely mouth!

*Why don't you slip into something? Paralysis or coma perhaps.*

'No sir, I was running high fever.' I lied subtly. I wanted to say had gone to see a prospective homosexual life-partner...waste of time, waste of energy.

'Yes of course, take ample leaves. What is the company's free health insurance for, after all, isn't it?' He said oozing sarcasm at every word.

*Oh that reminds me, the health insurance will also cover my anxiety medications that I will soon be a staple for me.*

'Sir, this is really the first time that my files are incomplete. You can ask Rakesh sir.' I pointed to our current branch manager so he could take a stand for me. He was the witness of endless hours of uncomplaining and unpaid overtime I put into my work.

'It is becoming so difficult to supervise everyone that you sometimes don't realize when they leave their work incomplete,' he spoke, smiling and showing his tiny teeth and big gums. Horror of the horrors.

*Yeah right. It must be so tough supervising someone who works harder than you.* His double standard was not a double shocker. I swore to never ever complete his share of the work.

'Next time if I find your files incomplete, then please, take a permanent leave of absence.' Rudra said sharply. I felt like rumbling his neat hair spikes into a mess.

Soon after that he left without checking anyone else's files. I felt like a kid whose incomplete homework was caught by the class teacher and everyone else go scot free.

'GOSH, DID YOU just look at him?' Jhanvi interrupted as she approached us with a box of sweets and a stack of expensive brown coloured envelopes.

'Did you hear him speak from that uber sexy mouth? He was giving me the butterflies.' Pooja blushed.

'What an excellent taste in fashion! His grey trouser was such a neat fit! Not one bling thing on his body. Was he wearing a Tag?' enquired Jhanvi.

'Rado.' Ajay was quick to respond.

I was like hello, this is the guy who insulted your esteemed colleague a few minutes ago.

'I want to gift exactly the same watch to my husband on our wedding night. Where can I get?' Jhanvi asked. Now this is the thing with girls. You show them one good thing and they will hunt down the supplier.

'You brought sweets? Anything special?' I said as I took the box of sweets from her hands to divert the attention from Mr Clooney who had just given me a sound beating.

'Oh yeah, this is my wedding invite and all of you have to be at the Krushimangal Hall next Sunday. No excuses. And yes, gifts are mandatory,' Jhanvi said.

I almost dropped the laddu as we three stared at her.

'*Arey baba*, just joking. No gifts please.'

'Why? Is Laxmi Mittal sponsoring your wedding?' Ajay asked as he picked up three laddus with one hand and kept the other hand free to eat them. *Boys will be boys!*

'No *re*...people will do what I did to them. They will bring gifts from their unwanted stock like the ones received on their marriage. Trash.' Her voice trailed off.

'So you mean no gifts. Only cash.' It started to make sense to me.

She laughed in response.

'Perks of being a CA. Smart,' Pooja replied. 'Anyway, are you going to invite Rudra?' We turned to look at her. 'I mean Rudra sir.' She blushed. She did this purposely. She already made her claim on the new boss and now she wanted all of us to tease her with him, such cheap stunts.

'Yaar, I really want to but I have met him just today. Is it appropriate to invite him? What will he think?' pondered Jhanvi.

'Look woman, you are getting married and I am still single. You better invite him or else I will tell everyone that no gifts and no cash.' Pooja said dangerously enough for Jhanvi to succumb as she dusted her greasy hands.

'SAVITA BEN, WHAT is that?' I asked my maid keeping my voice terrifyingly low as I slumped on the sofa trying to forget the bad day at work. I accidently walked all over the damp floor leaving my dirty footprints behind.

'What is what?' she asked frustrated as she dipped the rag into a bucket of water to mop the floor again. 'See what you did. How many times do I have to clean? Even I have children, I have to go home.'

What did I just ask and what was she venting.

'What are you wiping the floor with?' I asked, trying to soothe her nerves.

'This?' she lifted my t-shirt.

'Mom!' I screamed. 'Mom!!' This time louder.

'Why are you screaming?' My mom asked irritated as she emerged from the kitchen with a bhindi-stuck spatula in her hand.

'Why did you give Savita ben my t-shirt for wiping the floor without my permission?' I was still loud.

'Oh ho...because it was faded and looking old,' she said.

'Faded? You think that my Levi's t-shirt is faded? This is the latest fashion. I got this last week for two thousand bucks and now you have dipped it in this stinking phenyl water to clean your floor?' I slapped my palm over my head.

'What? Two thousand rupees! You spend your money on things like these? These old t-shirts? I can buy four saris in that price. *Arey* you can become a paid member on shaadi.com for that amount.' Clearly my mom didn't understand the difference between a Levi's and a rag.

When I did not react to that, she said huffing away, 'Ok spend it. Spend it all. But remember one thing, little droplets make a vast ocean. If you can't save now, then how will you save after marriage? You are going nowhere in life.'

'Huh?!' I was baffled.

'Even my salary is not two thousand rupees.' Savita ben raised her eyebrows.

'The shopkeeper made a fool out of you. Take me with you tomorrow and I will get your money back,' mom said.

'Increase my salary to two thousand rupees or find someone else.' Savita ben spoke like a shrewd business woman, taking advantage of the chaos between me and mom.

'Savita ben, don't say a word. I increased your salary just two months back.' Mom pointed the spatula at her now.

I sneaked into my room intending to dig a hole to hide all my branded clothes in it.

'WHAT'S THIS?' I picked up a card decorated in a small *dulhan-doli.*

'Pinky's wedding card. Came by post today morning,' mom said with a serious expression.

'Pretty decoration, *na*?'

'We are not going,' she announced taking a boiled potato, imagining it to be Jaina maasi and peeling its skin.

'Mom, please. Get over it.' I said. I had not told her that 'the' Mr Dollarkumar was gay or else she would have told half the world by now out of sheer joy. 'It's sad that we don't want to be a part of somebody's happiness by making a lame excuse for not being there.'

'If you want to go, go! But don't force me,' mom retorted.

'Everyone will ask about you. What will I tell them?' I asked.

'Tell them anything. Tell them my diabetes was high. Tell them that I don't attend scheming-people's weddings.'

Being a diabetic patient was like the ultimate illness one can have – I could come home from office if my mom suddenly had high sugar levels or can skip tedious trainings or make excuses if the guys I meet for wedding are not good enough. Actually I used this excuse to bunk classes in both school and college, way before my mom had diabetes.

'Fine, don't come. Then don't mind when people don't show up at my wedding,' I said, emotionally blackmailing her.

The only thing that terrified my mom the most was that no one would come to my wedding.

'Ok I will come, but then don't ask me to talk to them. I will taunt her at least once. We will go in the morning and return back at night. No overnight stay.'

I laughed 'Yeah please taunt her. She needs one. But just come ok. I am making reservations.'

'Not going to give more than hundred and one rupees in the

envelope, you just watch,' she said more to herself but loud enough for me to hear too.

'WHAT A NICE guy Jaina has selected for her daughter.' One of my distant aunts exclaimed as she was having lunch with my mom. I stood there, silently watching the drama unfold, and in my mom's case, explode.

'Huh,' my mom grunted. There she goes. '*Arey* this guy is my find,' she said as if maasi took away her lottery prize. 'Jaina played tricks and trapped this guy or else my Nitya would have been standing there on the stage next to him,' she said with a sour expression.

The excitement levels of my aunt rose, 'Arey Hema, what are telling?' She pressed for more details in her amazing Gujju English.

'Then what?' My mom fed her curiosity. 'Holding both my ears, I will never take any relatives who have young daughters, with me when we meet guys for my Nitya.'

'But we are not like that.' Kokila aunty felt offended as she took a bite of the samosa.

'No no, Kokila ben, not talking about you. Only these people are like that. If you have any nice guy in mind, do let me know for Nitya.' She tried her networking skills.

We saw Jaina maasi approaching from a distance towards us with hot *puris*. My mom turned away her face intentionally.

'What Hema? Why there is nothing in your plate?' She said pointing to my mom's plate filled with two of each roti and puri, and almost all varieties of vegetables from the plant kingdom. 'Here have this hot puri, specially for you,' she said as she tried to adjust it in her plate.

Our Hema ben pretended that she did not hear. Jaina maasi called her twice. This time I had to butt in, 'Mom, Jaina maasi is calling you,' I said pulling her sari's pallu.

'Oh, I didn't see you,' my mom said innocently to Jaina maasi who stood right before her.

'I was telling...have some puri,' Jaina maasi said, relieved that she finally had my mom's attention.

'Why Jaina? Got your Pinky married to the US guy I found and you don't have time to come to my place to invite me personally?' My mom asked curtly. Jaina maasi looked petrified.

'Now if Dollarkumar liked her, then what can we do? You get whatever is in your destiny.' Jaina maasi blamed destiny.

'Maasi, Pinky is on stage *na*? Come, I will wish her,' I said to ease the tension.

Maasi exhaled comfort. 'Yeah she was asking for you. I will take you there.'

'Hey, Congrats Pinks.' I exclaimed as I hugged her. 'Congrats Dollar!'

'Thanks,' they said.

'So married and all huh?' I smiled. 'Looking so pretty.'

I sat next to her on an empty sofa decorated with a shiny golden fabric.

'Thanks. I will post pictures and tag you,' she said adjusting her nose ring which kept falling.

'I am so surprised that maasa and maasi accepted him,' I told her.

'Means?'

'I mean, how did they react when you told them that he is gay?' I whispered in her ears.

'Err…actually. I haven't told them,' Pinky whispered right back.

'What! Why?' I said shocked. Then I looked at Jaina maasi who was boasting about her American son-in-law to the crowd. I felt bad for her.

'They won't understand.'

'But Pinks, I want you to be happy.'

'Going to the US makes me happy. Please don't tell them anything, I will tell them at the right time,' she said with hope in her eyes.

'I won't.' I pretended to smile through pressed lips.

'Mother promise?' She tugged at the skin of her throat.

'Yeah, mother promise.' I aped her.

A few minutes later, I exchanged my seat with Jaina maasi and handed her the bag with all the envelopes with money and the gifts they had got.

MONALI BHABHI AND I were standing near the *pani puri* stall when the videographer came there with his camera. We pretended to be busy but giving our most natural pose as he scrolled through us.

'Come bhabhi, we have to hide Dollarkumar's shoes,' I said washing my hands with a glass of water on an open ground.

'Let's hide his condom pack tonight instead of his shoes; we will earn lakhs,' she laughed.

'*Naa* they won't be needing condoms anyway,' I said absentmindedly.

'Why? Is she going to take morning-after pill?' Bhabhi asked me innocently.

'Yeah something like that. You want *hajmola*?' I changed the topic quickly.

'Hello Nitya beta? How are you?' Suresh uncle approached me.

'Oh Suresh uncle, I am fine. How are you?' I smiled and touched his feet. He blessed me.

'After Pinky, it's your turn now. Started looking or not?' He inquired.

'Yes, I have seen a few.'

'Good, good. What's your age?'

'I turned twenty-five two months back,' I said

'Twenty-five?' he repeated like it was going to change if he said it any louder. The way he asked was like I was sixty finding a groom of thirty. 'You have to be fast now. Most of the good guys are gone,' he said.

I really felt like telling him that the groom Pinky is marrying is gay. That would shift his concern from me to her.

'Kailash bhai, this is Nitya, a CA and very intelligent. Working in a top position at Axis bank,' Suresh uncle introduced me to another uncle.

'Beta, this is Kailash bhai. A very renowned stock broker. He is also from Surat.'

'*Kem chho* uncle?' I folded my hands.

'*Majama* beta, *saaru chhe.*'

The uncle went on to ask me my whereabouts, education and family details.

'Ok uncle, I have to go. Have to hide the groom's shoes. It was nice meeting you.' I excused myself.

'You know what happened at Pinky's wedding?' My mom asked me when I came back from work the next day.

'What?'

'Jaina gave her bag to someone to mind the cash and jewellery at Pinky's *bidai* and that person disappeared with all the valuables. They searched everywhere. Some say that it has to be an insider's job only.'

'That's terrible. Did they inform the police?'

'Now even police can't do much in this case. *Bechari Jaina*,' my mom exclaimed. I was so surprised. On the one hand she hated her, and on the other, she empathized. I learnt a lesson. Never try to sort out matters between two ladies. They will get together after a fight and you will be sidelined.

'Anyway, there is a good news also. Some Kailash bhai saw you at the wedding and liked you a lot for his son. They want to arrange a meeting on this Saturday.'

'Oh that is why he interrogated me. Saturday is fine. I will take half day off.' I said heating my food in the microwave.

# Our Family Members are Very 'Impotent'

Kailash uncle's son was a B.Com pass who was now into stock market. They had recently opened a new office on the sixth floor of the high rise Jolly Plaza, a well-known commercial building. While we were in the lift, mom instructed me to chant Shree Krishna mantra three times before I begin my meeting, like we do before writing an answer paper.

'*Kem chho*? *Aao, aao*.' Kailash uncle greeted us with a smile at the door.

He wore one gold bracelet and a golden watch on his left hand and a red sacred thread on his right. I could see a thick gold chain peeping out from his shirt. He looked like Bappi Lahiri's brother. Gujjus can be as insecure with a bling on their body as without their tiffin on long journeys.

I looked around. The infrastructure of his office was very modern and every piece of furniture had dark mango-wood finish. It smelt of fresh paint. Glass walls separated the cabins. A 40-inch plasma continuously displayed BSE Index on the silent mode.

My prospective mother-in-law wore more gold than any living human on the planet and looked like an incarnation of goddess Laxmi herself. She indicated us to sit on an expensive sofa. My mom gestured me to sit next to his mom. So I sat sandwiched between the two moms like an obedient child.

'Did you find any difficulty reaching this place?' His mom asked pouring water into two silver glasses.

'No, no, we have been here in this building before, for the inauguration of my niece's dental clinic on the first floor,' said my mom.

'We have one and only one son. No daughter. After we go, everything belongs to our Jig-ness. His father has set up this new *hoffis* for him only.' She meant office. Now I see why they arranged the meeting here. Mom and I soaked in every bit of information.

Apparently one and only one son in a matrimonial market is quite a catch. No additional sisters-in-law or brothers-in-law to give you a bad time during property division.

'We don't want any *dehaj-vehaj* from our to be daughter-in-law. We just want a nice *sanskari bahu* for our Jig-ness,' his father cleared. My mom gave a reaction like her prayers were answered.

'We are a very close-knit family and all our family members are very *impotent* to us. We only want the girl to adjust with everyone,' his mother added.

*Impotent*? She meant important. All family members are *impotent*. If I ever plan to get married to Jig-ness, then he has some very serious explaining to do.

'See we are middle-class working people. What we want for our daughter is her happiness. Nothing comes above that. We want a nice family and a good boy,' my mom said and they gave an understanding nod.

His mom disappeared into what seemed like a mini-kitchen and returned with two silver plates and silver spoons. *One more chance to show-off her silverware.* Two types of dhoklas were placed with two types of *chivra* and *kaju katli* topped with a silver leaf and some coconut chutney to go with. Yeah, dhokla is our staple diet.

'You really did not have to take the trouble and we already had our dinner,' my mom said as she dug into one of the dhokla pieces.

'Have this white dhokla. It really tastes good,' my mom told me as she finished hers. I felt so embarrassed. I can't eat at a guy's home. I can't take the risk of getting something stuck in my teeth.

'No, I am full.' I spoke between clenched teeth.

'*Arey* at least try. It's so soft,' she embarrassed me even more. I glared at my mom with a tight-lipped smile.

'No problem. If you don't like dhoklas, have some other *snakes*,' his mom told pushing a plate towards me.

I helped myself with a little chivra.

'Ae Jigla, Jigla!!' his father called out for his son.

So Jigla comes with a blackberry in one hand and an iPhone on his right ear. And yeah, you guessed it. Like-father like-mother and like-son, loaded with gold. In fact, he went one step ahead by wearing a gold earring in one ear. One can say that this family truly received Lord Tirupati's blessings. He wore a dark blue Hilfiger t-shirt with lighter blue denims.

He was on a call and signalled us that it will take him a couple of minutes. 'This is a very good time for investment Keshu bhai. Don't look, just jump. Five hundred in TATA, thousand in Birla and fifteen hundred in Sun Pharma,' he said with his eyes glued to the screen. Actually he looked quite attractive if you ignored his speech.

'Sorry aunty, I am new to this *bij-ness* so I stay a little *bi-jy,*' he said and my face fell.

We gave each other a brief nod of recognition. We were asked to sit in one of the cabins with glass walls to talk in private.

'So your work keeps you very busy?' I initiated the conversation.

'Yeah, but I am new in *bij-ness* so I have to learn. After few years, it will be okay. No *ten-sun,*' he said. He seemed jovial.

'What about you?' He asked.

'I am a Chartered Accountant and I spend most of my time filing returns,' I replied.

'Oh so you are the guys who convert black money into white,' he asked grinning like he had caught a naughty child peeing in a flower pot.

'Yes, we are the ones,' I said as a matter of pride.

'Hey, I have this issue where I bought a piece of land with the profit I made from my dummy company. Is there any way I can be exempted from tax?' he asked.

Here we are discussing our matrimony. This is what happens when a Gujju stock broker meets someone from finance. They won't leave any chance to a viable profit. 'We have been taught *bij-ness* since birth,' he explained.

'Sure. That *toh* I can do even in my sleep. We can tweak some laws, make false invoices and you are good to go.' I said with a confidence like it was the easiest thing in the world to do.

He beamed with joy. So much so that he could have married me right there in exchange for a money-saving tip.

'You seem to be good at business. Have you ever considered going for MBA?' I asked.

'Arey, why to spend money on a top B-school *phee*-school when you can learn here, for free. *Bij-ness* is in my blood. It was even in my grandfather's blood and great grandfather's blood,' he said like he was a descendent of blue blooded Henry Ford or something.

*Bij-ness is a bloody hereditary disease. Got it.*

'My father asked me *beta* what you want to do after twelve standard? I said I want to do a white-collar job where I can sit in the AC and print money. So I joined his *bij-ness*. Easy life. *Majja ni* life.'

Then for the next few minutes, we talked some more about business and sensex and whitening money whilst forgetting our actual purpose. We totally lost track of time.

'How much are you guys going to talk?' His mom interrupted.

'*Bus* last five minutes.' He blinked five fingers.

'I think I should get going. Nice meeting you Jig-ness.' I smiled.

'Oh *pleej*, call me Jigs,' he said.

'So what you say? Ready for second meeting' he asked almost immediately. I liked his confidence. I liked the meeting too. It was a highly intellectual meeting without the stereotypical questions.

'My mom will let you guys know.' I smiled. 'And here is my card. If you need any help with invoices. I can give you a twenty percent discount on my fees.' I laughed. Twenty minutes with Jigs and the Gujju in me was coming out.

'It's not safe for you ladies people to travel alone this late. No *poblem.* My *diver* will drop you home,' his father said as me and mom stood up to leave.

'SHOULD I CALL them for a second meeting?' My mom looked at me expectantly.

'He is a nice guy but not my type. I want to keep looking,' I replied.

She looked at me in horror. The drama was building up. One can only imagine what was going to happen next.

'Not...your...type?' The pitch of her voice increased with every word.

I quickly closed the main door and windows to cushion her screams. I did not want to entertain our nosy neighbours.

'He is too Gujju for me. Moreover, he is just B.Com and you know, the share market is a risky business. You know what happened to Harshad Mehta and Ketan Parekh. Who knows, he could be the next.' I managed to say everything in one go. I might not have gotten the chance to speak again.

'You think that in this recession, stable jobs are not risky? At least in Jignesh's case, he has his father for support,' she said with hope.

'Can we just drop this?' I asked frustrated.

'If you do all these *nakhras* no, you are not going to get any guy. Learn to let minor things go,' she stormed out of my room. I took a deep breath.

Maybe she was right. Yes he was a little Gujju, but then, even I am short. He is good-looking, logical, sounds honest, family seems loving (and rich) and above all, he was cheerful. But the thing with arranged marriage is that one always feels the next one would be better.

THERE IS NO greater agony for a woman than bearing an untold story inside her. I conference-called Komal and Malvika.

'How are the meetings coming along?' Malvika asked.

'They are like speed dating,' I replied and narrated the Jig-ness incident.

'If you didn't like him then why didn't you *rape* up the meeting soon?' said Komal pulling my leg.

'Very funny!' I kept a neutral tone.

'And Nitya, you shouldn't hurt his *fillings*,' Malvika said and this time everyone laughed.

My friends are clowns, I tell you. Instantly the grief-stricken atmosphere of my home turned to comedy circus. *What would I do without them?*

'How did he look, by the way?' Malvika was all curious. For her, any guy lesser in looks than Shahid Kapoor was not worth looking at.

'Good looking actually. And he was very interesting. That guy really knew his stuff,' I answered.

'And if you think that only the south Indian possessed all the gold of India, then you're mistaken my friend. This family could easily outshine them,' I added.

'The thing is that I am not looking for everything in every department, but I want at least something in every department,' I said.

'How can you even think of departing with a gold mine just like that? You are such a gone case,' Komal said, and I hated to admit, but she was right. With that amount of gold I could build three golden temples in Amritsar.

'With friends like you, who needs riches?' I lied cheesily. Everyone needs both friends and riches.

'HOW WAS YOUR weekend?' Ajay inquired as we passed from one food counter to another, overloading our plates with some unpronounceable delicacies at Jhanvi's wedding.

'Weekend huh?' I said frustrated. 'I got at least seven rishta aunties asking beta when are you getting married and four younger cousins saying didi get married fast. We are in queue. Everyone is a matchmaker these days. I am so sure that this shaadi.com is owned by an aunty.'

Ajay let out a chuckle 'Yeah I know how wedding seasons can be. It's horrible. Last to last week, I had some uncles inquiring about my salary package to determine if I am ready to settle down or not. You see the general criteria are always the age for girls and income for guys.'

'I got asked about me at a funeral once. Beat that,' I said.

'Funeral?' he almost choked on his food. 'You are joking, who does that?'

'*Toh kya*? These days it is becoming even harder to dodge relatives. They wrapped up the sobbing part in half hour neat and then very conveniently, the topic steered to more interesting things like my wedding for one.' I said as we stood on the live counter waiting for the cook to serve steaming dosa directly onto our plates.

'Urmila maami, my mother's grand uncle's daughter-in-law told my mom how that grand uncle had just one last wish...to see me wedded. Could you believe that?' I jerked my head to express anger. 'As such, he kept forgetting things but never forgot about my wedding. Talk about old age.'

'Grand uncle must have told that to every parent with children of marriageable age in your family. He was probably playing that I-will-be-gone-any-minute card.'

'Exactly! You see, he has five children. Each one of them has two to three off springs. Out of which about nine or ten are married. So in his family alone he has compassed about sixteen weddings, including one of his great grandchildren. But no, still Nitya's wedding is still left.' I said explaining our complicated compounded hierarchy. We do not have a family tree, we have family forests.

'Newlyweds fell for his baby-making trap,' I said.

Ajay looked at me questioningly.

'The usual. I am too old. My last wish is to play with my great-grandchildren thing.' I elaborated as I dug into the dosas. 'He has, like, five great grandchildren. At this age, how much is he going to play?'

'You won't believe it, the other day I met a girl for matrimony. You know what happened? She said she didn't like men who dictate women. For example, she said, I like mini-skirts and I am going to wear them after marriage too. I said of course you can. In fact, I like girls in mini-skirts. She gave me a dirty look and said that she did not like guys staring at her bare legs.'

I laughed out loud, 'Crazy. What happened then?'

'What else will happen? She said that I was a pervert and rejected me.'

'Ha ha ha! Oh my god!' I kept laughing.

Ajay just smiled. 'You are looking pretty today, by the way,' he complimented without making an eye contact.

'Thanks. It's just this violet sari. I get plenty of compliments whenever I wear it.' I tried to be modest.

'No. It's you who makes the sari look hotter,' he said, 'better, I mean... better,' he corrected himself quickly, fiddling with the string of noodles, his eyes looking somewhere distant.

He sounded like the sales guy trying to woo women into buying saris. These were one of the lousiest words I had heard but the admiration in his eyes was genuine when I finally had the chance to look into them.

'*Mehendi laga ke rakhna... doli saja ke rakhna...*' Pooja came along humming the song in the background. 'I am so going to play this song on my wedding.'

She wore a wine-red sari with a black backless blouse and six inch stilettos which made her tower over every girl and guy present at the venue. I looked like a minion in front of her.

'You look good,' I faked a compliment. 'Found any *dulha*? Look around, someone somewhere is made for you,' I winked at her.

'The one I have my eyes on is already here,' she said coyly.

'Who? That dork Tejas from Valsad branch? I knew it. I always had my doubt that you have a thing with him,' Ajay said as he wiped the red gravy stains from his crisp white shirt with a tissue, spreading it even more.

'Oh please. My taste in men is way too high. I am talking about Rudra Desai,' she said pointing her chin in his direction.

'Shit. He made it to the wedding. And now he is making his way here.' I was desperately searching for a place to hide.

'Good evening everyone,' he spoke to the two of them. 'Good evening Nitya Trivedi,' he gave his trademark smile. The one which can make women like Pooja and Jhanvi go weak in their knees.

*Oh wait a minute, did he call me by my name? He remembers my name?!*

'Good evening sir,' we all said in chorus. I skipped the word 'sir'. He wore a grey shirt with thinly spaced black stripes stitched to perfection and yet another expensive watch to match. His hair was carefully gelled back and he resembled the handsome bad guy you see in some daily soaps.

'So our valuable colleague Jhanvi will be on leave for three weeks, which means that all her pending and non-pending work will be distributed amongst your team,' he talked business. Pooja turned beet red when he looked at her. Even his inhumanity would feel like music to her ears.

'You guys will have to audit her Central mall, M D Patel and Karanjidas files, and in addition to that, we have two more new audits coming up. It is going to be a busy month,' he said addressing us like the waiters in the wedding.

'Oh yes, I will. I mean we will sir, we will complete it before three weeks,' Pooja spoke for all of us. When it came to making fake promises, she goes an extra mile.

Good for me though. Now that she had committed, it was her responsibility to get the job done.

I maintained a dignified silence all the while. Actually, I was ignoring him and he too was hardly paying enough attention to notice that I was ignoring him. He acted like I didn't exist at all.

'Pooja, Ajay, let's go and meet Jhanvi,' I said tugging at Pooja's hand.

At this point he saw me and quickly glanced at me from head to toe. I could not tell if he was checking me out or what.

'Did you finish your pending tasks, Nitya?' He asked and gave a half-lip smile.

*Was he mocking me? Was he sorry for shouting at me that day?*

'Yes sir, I have,' I said confidently. 'In fact, I had some time on hand and I knew that Jhanvi is going to take a leave so I have already started my work on Karanjidas file, which will be completed sooner than expected.'

I saw a hint of appreciation in his eyes.

'Very well. See you guys tomorrow.' He left as our ex-boss Rakesh sir called him to collect a plate for himself.

No words of appreciation from him. I wanted to hear the words. Girls need words. They are audio species just as the guys are visual.

My body burned with revenge. Thanks to Ajay, I knew that he drove a Range Rover. Show off *kahinka*. How difficult can it be to find a Range Rover in a parking lot of an average wedding hall where average people come in average cars? Let's teach him a lesson.

'AWW YOU LOOK so pretty honey, congratulations.' I said hugging Jhanvi on stage.

'By the way, do you accept cash or check?' Ajay teased her.

'Oh just so you know that we are chartered accountants and good investors too. So if you need any help with all the crores and the black money you are going to earn from this wedding, we have a good investment scheme,' I offered.

'You guys,' she started laughing. 'You all ate properly *na*?'

'A lot. Can't eat for the next eight years. Enjoy your honeymoon and don't worry about work. Pooja will finish it before three weeks, isn't it Pooja?' I spoke through gritted teeth.

'Oh and I have invited Rudra sir. Did you meet him?' Jhanvi asked Pooja.

'She was all over him. She is going to take him home,' said Ajay.

'I am fast, you see. Before any other woman lays her claws over him, I will,' she said

'Anyway, we are getting late. See you,' said Ajay tapping his watch.

'WHAT HAPPENED SIR? Everything ok?' Pooja touched Rudra's shoulder as we reached the parking lot. *Unnecessary body contact.*

'Nothing much. I got a flat tyre,' he said looking sharply at me. I felt a little jolt. *Does he know?*

'Such a big car, don't you have a spare tyre?' I passed a cutting word, still not referring to him as 'sir'. I was savouring the moment.

'Actually, I have one. But you see, I've got a puncture in all four tyres, co-incidentally.' He tilted his head to one side, still talking to me alone. I wanted to feel satisfied by the revenge but now I was damn scared. I tried to keep a neutral expression.

'Sir, this car is a beast, seventeen point six mileage, eight speed transmission. Surely some wantons out there must have done this. I can take you to the nearest garage on my bike.' Ajay offered help.

'Are you going home alone?' he asked Ajay.

'I have to give lift to Pooja. This farmhouse is on the outskirts, so getting an auto can be very difficult'

'No problem. You go home with her. Anyway, we will have to come back with mechanic triple seat. Nitya will give me a lift in her car,' he said giving me a deadly glance. He didn't ask me whether I was going to give him a lift; he told me. He looked way hotter when angry. Even before he finished his sentence, I already knew that he knew that I had punctured the tyres, all four of them.

Pooja shifted her weight uneasily to her other leg. 'Sir, we can wait for you,' she said determined, dreading that I would be left alone with him.

'That's ok Pooja. You guys carry on. You have to be at the office on time tomorrow. Nitya can leave as soon as she drops me and the mechanic back here,' he told her without even looking in my direction.

I DROVE SLOWLY, scanning every shop we crossed, desperate to find a mechanic so I could get rid of Rudra. I could stand him no more. *How will I stand him ten hours in office tomorrow?*

From the corner of my eye I could see that he kept looking in my direction every few seconds.

'Yes sir?' I matched his gaze roughly the next time he looked at me in order to keep him from staring anymore.

'Why did you do it?' He asked amused.

'I didn't do it,' I replied panic-stricken. 'I mean, do what sir?' I tried to control the damage done. My heart pounded.

'All four tyres?' He laughed. 'Like seriously?'

Should I be relieved or was it the evil laughter before the storm?

'I don't know what you are talking about.' I denied taking responsibility, just like the Al-Qaeda group.

'You know exactly what I am talking about,' he said. 'You know the first day when I scolded you about your pending files?'

*How can I forget that? I still get nightmares about it.* I looked at him and blinked.

'I didn't want to give any wrong impression to anyone taking me for a troll with their lax attitude towards work. That is my working style.'

I halted near a garage. 'Sir, you can check here.'

Unfortunately the mechanic there had just left. Every garage we went to turned us down. My luck was not working. Maybe I should have forwarded those chain emails ensuring god's blessings.

'I am really getting late. My mom must be worried,' I said checking my phone every two minutes for exaggeration.

'That you should have thought before you took your sweet revenge,' he spoke with a tight-lipped smile.

'Anyway, just drop me here. I think I will get an auto from the roundabout.'

'And what about your car?' I asked almost apologetically.

'It's a secure car park. I will send someone to collect it tomorrow morning,' he said and my heart melted. *He is not that bad after all.*

'Sir, I will drop you home. Where do you stay?' I had to repent.

'You sure? I stay at Athwagate. Is it very far from your place?'

'No, no...in my way,' I said and shifted into the fourth gear.

You don't necessarily have to like your boss, but you don't even have to hate him. One can always try to stay on neutral grounds.

# It's not You; it's Me

*Hi this is H-IT-ESH Joshi! Well, well, well, how do I describe myself? Here is a point based summary for an easy read.*

1. *An IT engineer, an evil Sagittarian, 81 born, hometown Rajkot. We are a family of one sister (who is married in Dubai and blessed me with an extremely cute and naughty niece), and the most loving parents in the universe.*

2. *I am very ambitious and want to be the world's biggest programmer. I work extremely hard each day which brings me closer to realizing my dreams.*

3. *I am a food-o-holic and staying in US makes me miss all the Indian food. I love to cook. In fact, all my friends call me a cooker for the same reason. So someone marrying me will not have to worry about fixing up a dinner for me. I will be more than happy to make a meal for her.*

4. *I don't believe in horoscope crap but my parents do. But if I really really like the girl, then this condition can be over-ruled.*

5. *I like to laugh a lot, I laugh at myself as well as others. I have a laughing fit about 40-50 times per day, but sometimes it may cross 100.*

6. *I want a partner who doesn't make a fuss about everything and is extremely easygoing.*

7. *I am looking for someone who respects me and my folks. She should get along with my buddies too as they are an indispensable part of my life. I firmly believe in bros before hoes (sorry for the language.)*

8. *The girl who marries me will be the happiest girl on the planet. She will be my princess and I will protect her like a knight in shining armour.*

WOW! IT WAS love at first page. This was one of the best profiles I had come across on shaadi.com. I pressed the interest button.

Five days later, I got his email.

*Hi Nitya,*

*Hitesh Joshi this side. You found me on shaadi.com and I am writing you an email with that reference. Sorry for late reply as I had been out of town and now I am trying to catch up with all the pending tasks.*

*Before I get some time to interact with and exchange all details, I just wanted to send my bio data first to acknowledge your response and move this process further.*

*I usually don't get so busy :) but since I am visiting India this February end, I got overloaded with work at office.*

*I will try to get back to you this weekend for some gup-shup :)*

*In the meantime, you can go through my biodata and feel free to contact me. Hope this works for now. Till then Chao!! :)*

*Thanks,*

*H-IT-ESH*

'H-IT-ESH?' Even his name has IT in it.

His email was devoid of any monotone and stood out. Somewhere in the heart of my hearts, I knew that there was going to be a connection with him.

THE FIRST THING I noticed in his face was his hundred volt smile. It reached his eyes and made them twinkle. He had a little stubble at his chin and his jet black hair was neatly combed to one side; not that *Champak Bhomiya* kind of hairdo, but that of a cute school boy. Though his skin was the darkest shade of black, his chilled attitude started to make an impression, the good one.

'Hey sorry *yaar*, I know it's too late in India, but this is the only time I get off from work,' he gave an explanation into the video chat. I liked his informal way of conversation.

'*Koi nai yaar.*' I smiled. '*Chalta hai.* It's OK.' I left my waist-length hair open. It was one of my key assets which I choose to feature whenever I can, proxy for my short height.

'I understand you have read my biodata.'

'Yes I have,' I said. I did not go all gaga about it. His profile totally floored me but I couldn't tell him that.

'And you?' I asked.

'Me too. I feel very uncomfortable speaking to a girl for matrimonial purpose without knowing about her a bit.'

'Tell me about it.' I raised my hands in the air to agree.

For the next fifteen minutes, we shared our experiences on how some disasters had happened in the past when we were set up on blind dates.

'This one time, my *mota pappa* set me up with this girl who was majorly religious. She told me that she wants to join the *brahmakumaris* and lead a life of a celibate but I clarified that I intend to consummate my marriage with my partner,' he said.

'No, you did not just say that.' My eyes widened in shock, 'How did she react?'

'I think she was going to pass out,' he laughed. 'She said that she was not interested to meet and all but her mom forced her, that is why she was there. Can you believe that?' he asked.

'My *maami* at Surendranagar has already promised to light five *diyas* of pure ghee at Saibaba temple whenever I get married,' he added.

'Yeah, yeah some people get married only for their *maami*, isn't it?' I teased him.

'Yes, only for my loving relatives because in India, your relatives are the only people who are more worried about your marriage than you yourself are,' he rolled his eyes.

'True that. Not only marriage, career too. In every social gathering, you will find surplus career-expert uncles. When I bagged this job, "what's you starting pay?", "how much you get in hand?", "joining *kab ki hai*" were the frequently asked questions,' I added.

'They keep asking me how to convert their black money into white. For free. They think that one Nitya in hand is worth two CAs in the bush. Freeloaders,' I said. He chuckled in the video. *Thank God for Skype!*

'Yeah and they think that all IT guys can repair computers. Last year when I was in Surendranagar, one uncle said *beta*, now that you are here, *zara virus nikal do aur lage haath* screen *bhi thik kar dena.* I said uncle I am a software programmer. I can't repair screens. He said what kind of engineer are you who couldn't fix things.'

'I know. Poor engineers are taken as handymen by default,' I agreed.

Who knew that hating relatives could bring two people closer!

'Acchha so tell me, what are you looking for in a guy?' he asked steering the topic.

'Hmm… one who understands the difference between eyeliner and mascara, concealer and primer, mauve and purple.' I counted three points on my fingers.

'Huh?' He sounded baffled.

'Relax, just kidding' I said giggling. I heard him take a breath. 'What about you?'

'In search of a girl who can clearly understand the difference between Star Trek and Star wars, bouncer and a yorker.'

'Huh?' I sounded stupid.

'Arey just joking yaar, relax,' he laughed.

'Ok tell me, pizza or pasta?' he rapid fired.

'None. I eat, dream and live Pav bhaji,' I replied.

'*Firangi* babe or *desi kudi*?' I asked next.

'Desi kudi any day with a little firang touch,' he was quick to reply.

I raised my eyebrows in appreciation of his choice.

'Rock, Jazz or country music?' He asked the next question.

'Full Bollywood masala,' I said proud of my Indian heritage. 'India or *Amreeka*?'

'Forty years in *Amreeka* and then back to roots.'

We kept chatting for the next hour, next week and the week after that. We used to talk during the time when I came from work and before I went to work the next day and in between. We had reached the stage of liking each other. Though we had not confessed this, but we knew it. Long before we started to exchange good morning, noon and night texts, but steered clear of 'non-veg' jokes.

'*CHAL NA BEY* Hitesh... let's go to the cheesecake factory,' one of his friends asked him laughing in the background one night as we Skyped. It had been two weeks and this was our seventh meeting.

'*Namaste bhabhiji*,' one of his room-mates folded his hands into the camera.

'*Raam raam*.' I smiled back at him.

'Am busy,' Hitesh answered him through gritted teeth. I think he mouthed 'Get lost' to him.

'Dude, then we will be watching that new Bollywood movie alone?'

'What?' Hitesh asked perplexed.

'*Arey*, the same one which has that hot item girl you are so fond of.' Another one asked loud enough for me to hear. I saw them laughing in the background.

'One sec.' Hitesh put me on hold and the voices in the background faded.

'Fuck off you guys,' he said to his friends who were making a mickey out of him. I heard it. Though the voice was too low, I heard it. I smiled like an idiot.

'*Item number aapka, faisla aapka, jago grahak jago*,' they guffawed in the background.

'*Dost dost naa raha...*,' another one sang as Hitesh shut his door.

'Don't mind *ya*. These jokers know that I am talking with a girl so...' he said a little embarrassed.

'That's ok... what else do they say about me? Tell me no,' I asked intrigued.

'Errr... my friend Bhavin Teshwala is a self-acclaimed rapper. He has composed a song about us. About me. That I have become a complete nutcase after I met you,' he said shyly.

'Really? I have a song? Read it. Or better, sing it' My anxiety rose.

'Errr...'

'Please, please, please.' I folded my hands.

'Ok.' He finally gave in. I think boys can't resist a girl who pleads three-four times in a baby voice. He drew out a book from somewhere.

*'Love, love, love,*
*Like cinnamon and clove,*
*His thoughts are interwove,*
*Nitya is his ladylove,*
*He has lost his sleep,*
*Cause Nitya is for keep,*
*Nitya is a bookcase,*
*Hitesh is her nutcase.'*

'Oh my god!' I laughed like a maniac.

'You liked it?' he asked expectantly.

'Umm...a little lame but I loved it. That is so sweet and so crazy. No one has ever written a song for me before. Say thanks to him,' I said. The poem was pathetic, but hey, someone had put in an effort.

'Did you hear the lyrics?' He asked cautiously.

'Yeah. Why?'

'So what do you think about *it*?'

'What is there to think about?'

'Nothing. Do one thing. I will mail you the song. I will rap it in my own voice. Listen to the song, read the lyrics again and again and again, and then tell me tomorrow what you think about the "it",' he said huskily. That was the first time he spoke to me in that voice. It was the sexiest voice I had ever heard. Ok not the sexiest. Rudra has the sexiest voice. But Hitesh's voice came pretty close to that.

I heard the song again and again and again, and I felt the jitters. I was linked to him. He was asking me how I felt about it. And I said that I did not understand. How stupid can I be! I was thinking of all the clever things I would say to him the next day and blushed like a fool.

Flirting and coyly trying to express feelings is the best when in a relationship.

'OH HI!' I tapped Rudra's shoulder when I ran into him at Big Bazaar, 'Rudra sir.'

He turned around. We greeted each other by removing our respective earphones.

'Nitya!' he looked pleasantly surprised. He paired a lemon yellow Diesel t-shirt with dark green straight fit chinos. His hair was neatly messy and he looked unbelievably sexy. 'What are you doing here?'

'Shopping sir. Salary credited today, na.' I grinned.

'Oh yeah right.' He raised his eyebrows in acknowledgment.

'Sir, you come here?' Funny to see your boss shopping around in retail stores just like you. I mean it is difficult to imagine your boss shop at the same places. It's like royalty meet peasant. He will pick the same brand of sugar and soap as you. No special privileges for him here.

'Actually I am here for a business meeting. I came to meet the finance manager of Big Bazaar. Talk him into giving his company accounts to our bank. Let's see now.' He picked up a basket and handed to me and then he picked one for himself.

'I will get something for home too now that I am here.' He produced a list from his back pocket and scrolled through the aisles without making an eye contact with me. His mother making him run down to the nearby kirana-wala to get groceries, embarrassing it is, naturally.

I savoured the moment.

'We will start from the left most aisle where the cleaning stuff is kept and then work our way through the groceries at the right in a snake like pattern, ok?' He made a shopping strategy.

'Ahan.' I nodded. Spending time with a boss has never hurt anyone. Maybe I can talk about my promotion. I am sure Ajay and Pooja would never miss this kind of an opportunity.

It is so sexy when a man takes charge. Not that I had to follow him or shop with him, but I was just curious to know what he picks up, an inside story of his life. Imagine if I tell this to Pooja at work, it will be a scoop. Like how glamorous Rudra Desai looked while buying a Mortien mat.

'So what other plans for weekend, sir?'

'My sister and brother-in-law are coming over to my place from Hyderabad,' he said while picking up a pack of six Surf detergents and placing it in his basket and crossing it off from his list. *Duh! Process!*

'You just have one sister? No brother?'

'Yup. She recently completed her paper and got her PhD in genetics. Now she is working as a research scientist.'

'A scientist! Wow! The dream of every Indian parent,' said I, with wide eyes of appreciation.

'Sir, try this body soap. This is the new collection in the market.' A sales girl picked up a soap from the promotions and handed it to Rudra.

Rudra shook his head.

'Sir, this has vitamin E and other beauty qualities, sir. It will make you fresh and glowing after a bath.' The sales girl was trying to meet her weekly targets. I felt she deliberately chose Rudra; it was not even a men's soap. He is just so drool-worthy.

We politely passed through her and reached another aisle.

'And you? Do you have any siblings?' He asked as we scanned the category for other household cleaning products. He placed a carton of phenyl in his basket. He looked so domestic. I picked up a box of tissues.

'Nope. Am a lone child.'

'Why chartered accountancy?' He asked me off guard.

'Why chartered accountancy?' I repeated his question. I thought of an intelligent answer but then told the truth. 'Hmm... I wanted to be a fashion designer. And the thought of her only daughter being a *darzi* put my mother off for weeks. She wanted me to be a doctor but given my low percentage in twelfth standard, we settled for a B.Com and then I went on to become a CA to make up.'

'*Darzi*?' He chuckled.

'A term parents give to an aspirant fashion designer hoping to drill some sense into them and picking a more suitable profession.' I jerked my head. 'At least it put an end to all the critic relatives who thought I was not going to get anywhere in life,' said I. 'But thereafter, I was introduced to a new breed of relatives who asked me, "*Beta CA ban gayi*? Now maintain my records for free".'

'Ha ha... This once I had a relative come up to me and ask *beta* from which university are you doing CA from?'

I couldn't stop myself from laughing mildly.

'And how did you end up being a branch manager? I mean you are so young for this post,' I asked him.

'We started from very humble beginnings. My father was an accountant in a textile company. So to afford my CA fees, I took up some tuition classes during my B.Com and worked my way up to pass all the CA modules in my first attempt, and the best part is, that I got a very good mentor when I was doing my articleship. He guided me and I became a branch manager quickly. He is my guru; I owe him everything. He means a lot me.'

'Hmm.' I nodded my head. I always knew that he is one intellectual badass. I took up a packet of biscuits with cream and began to read the ingredients.

'You're a vegetarian?' he asked.

I noticed that he was looking at me while I read the ingredients. 'Yeah, pure vegetarian. Don't even eat eggs. My family members *toh* even avoid going to restaurants where they serve both veg and non-veg food for the fear that the chef might be using the same vessels to cook their meals in.' I explained.

Two girls passed by, one of them pointing her chin in Rudra's direction. She whispered something in another's ear and then they started blushing. Thankfully this went unnoticed with him.

'So are you committed?' He asked me.

*That's a very personal question.*

'Umm...no. Why?' I know he asked casually and there are no answers to some whys. But sometimes it's fun observing someone in an awkward situation.

'Generally...Is your family looking for a groom for you?'

'Yeah. I have seen a couple of guys but didn't like them much,' I replied. Ok I skipped the part where a couple of guys rejected me too. Underestimating your own worth allows others to ignore your value. He is my boss, not Komal or Malvika with whom I can have a heart-to-heart.

Meanwhile two ladies in the baking aisle were fighting over a last pack of a readymade cake mix. It was like watching a wildlife documentary.

'And what about you?' I queried.

'I was dragged to see a girl two days back at knife point.'

'Knife point?' I chuckled.

'My mum…'

'I understand how compelling parents can get.'

'Didn't like the girl though. She showed her Facebook profile pictures in a private meeting, showing off how she fell into the "hundred likes profile picture club".'

I was enjoying our supermarket stroll.

Rudra picked up various biscuits and readymade cakes and chocolates and chips. It is so cute when a grown up man still likes to eat all nursery and kindergarten food.

He talked about how he got into the company and how he was thinking about his next promotion only after recently being promoted. I casually mentioned how I deserve a promotion.

We waited in the never-ending queue to pay the bill.

'Someone please open the second counter. Just look at the queue,' I shouted from the back. All the other people in front of me joined the protests.

'Rohit, Premal… open another counter. The queue is getting longer.' A guy shrieked to the two other staff members, who were busy doing nothing and tried to act dumb. One of them picked up a broom and started to sweep the floor though it was not dirty. *Work politics!* Some colleagues will choose to do sit idle and stare in vacuum rather than share your work.

'What to do madam? There is no free staff,' came the reply from the guy at the till.

'And that is why they should lay off such burdens,' Rudra expressed his disappointment.

'You know you should always love your work but not your company. I don't mean that you should not love your company but your loyalty should be more towards you work,' he said as a matter of fact. 'Tomorrow if the company makes profits, then on the annual speech they will say that because of you employees we are here. But if the company incurs loss, they would not think twice before laying you off,' he said, enlightening me.

'Sir, is our company laying off?' I asked tensed. Was he sending me an indirect message? My job is surely in danger. And suddenly I began to miss the traffic-jammed office routes which I used to curse each morning.

'No no! This is just a thought. Don't worry, we are not making anyone redundant,' he said assuring. I took a deep breath.

He paid the bill in cash and I produced my meal card.

'Where the way to a man's heart is cooking, the way to a woman's heart is shopping,' I said slinging my bag on my back.

We walked towards the parking lot and saw various food stalls.

'You want to eat something?' He pointed towards the stalls of pani puri and pizzas.

'Umm...Ok I will have a pani puri. They make it with mineral water here.'

'I am going to eat a whole pizza with all the side orders. Pan flavoured ice-cream, paneer tikka pizza. Can't do without an Indian touch,' he said producing a wallet.

'Token sir,' the brawny stall wala asked him as he told us to make way for his other customers waiting with a leaf bowl for pani-puri. He mechanically put aloo fillings and dipped it in first spicy water and then sweet water and then directly into the bowl.

The self-dependent ethical woman in me started to pay for my pani puri. Rudra almost grabbed the wallet from me.

'What are you doing?' he said and took two tokens. One for my pani puri and other for his pizza.

'Thanks for the pani puri, sir,' I said dumping the leaf bowl in a dustbin and washing my hands with a mug of water kept beside it.

He produced a pack of cigarettes and lit one of them. I tried to avoid the surprise on my face.

'I was a chain smoker once, but now I am trying to quit,' he said dragging two puffs from the newly-lit cigarette and stubbing the remaining under his shoes. 'This is just to satisfy that burning need sometimes.'

'Thinking of implanting another special set of lungs in my body so that I can continue my special smoking habits,' he added with a grin.

I smiled.

'Remember that day when you punctured my car?' He said. I turned beet red. 'Actually a very close friend of mine stayed nearby and I could have crashed at his place that night. But I didn't.'

I looked up with my eyes demanding an answer.

'Because I wanted to ride with you to know you better,' he replied.

The shock I felt was greater than any earthquake measured on a Richter scale. His eyes looked legitimate. How inappropriate! I was lost for words. Was he sending me some kind of signal?

He was delighting in my stunned expression.

'Ok then, see you tomorrow,' he said giving me a sly grin before he sped off. I stood like the Statue of Liberty. *Is Rudra Desai, the 'hunk of the hunks' hitting on me?*

I LAY ON the sofa in shorts on a lazy Sunday, texting Hitesh. I shook my head, giggling all alone at his replies.

I stopped when I realized that my mom was watching me with hawk eyes. I put my phone on silent mode and casually picked up a newspaper.

'Who is it?' She asked me suspiciously.

'No one. Forwarded message,' I said hiding my face in the newspaper.

'Do you have a boyfriend?'

'What! No!' I said.

'Then why are you smiling?' Her suspicions grew stronger.

'Why? Can't people smile? Should I cry then?'

'Our neighbour Hansa aunty's daughter was also smiling a lot on the phone. What happened? Her mother did not control her so she ran away with some guy. Poor woman, she has not been able to set her foot in the temple since. But I am not like her. I know how to control you and your secret smiles.'

I slapped my forehead.

'My messages are not secret. They are just private.'

'*Haan haan* secret, private... same thing only,' she said. 'You think I don't know that you are talking to that black boy.'

'Hitesh,' I said firmly.

'What do you like in him? Can't you find any fair and smooth guy, like cotton?'

'Cotton? Georgette? Banarasi Silk? He is my potential husband, not a sari,' I retorted angrily.

'Did you ask when he is coming from America? If you wait for him, then all the good guys will go. I know you have stopped talking to others. Full day you are on phone with him. Your marriage is not fixed yet, be careful.'

'Ma, he is a thousand times better and smarter than the morons Pappu uncle has been showing,' I replied.

'These days children are too spoilt. I didn't utter a single word when your grandparents fixed my marriage.'

'And what is this?' Mom slapped my bare thigh. 'Buy a full pant.'

I stood up and walked out of the room.

I PICKED UP Hitesh's call in half a ring. 'You know you are the most gorgeous girl I have ever talked to.'

'No hi, no hello, *seedha* compliments? What's up mister?' I asked, amused.

'What do you like in me by the way?' I said quickly. *Never ever distract a guy when he is complimenting you.*

'Umm ... too many. Your eyebrows for one.'

'Eyebrows? Very funny.' I made a face even if he couldn't see me.

'No really,' he tried to pull a bad joke too far, 'and such cute ears.'

'Please learn how to flirt.' I said, totally un-amused.

'Learn? Huh,' he said with an air of confidence, 'I give crash courses in that, baby.'

'*Waise*, I am not too bad myself. Don't you want a tall Amitabh Bachchan in your short Jaya Bachchan family?' he asked casually suppressing his laughter.

'Why? Don't you want some white milk in your black tea colour family?' I counter-replied.

'*Ha ha ha,*' he crowed, 'such a smart mouth.'

'Why have you called? I don't have much time. *Jaldi bol*,' I *bhao-khao-ed.*

'Aww you felt bad.'

'Heard the song I sent you?' His tone suddenly changed from funny to seductive in a milli-second. *How does he do that?*

Yesterday he sang '*hume tumse pyaar kitna*', taped it and sent it to me.

'Yeah nice song. You sing melodiously,' I said very casually, suppressing my joy.

'And the lyrics?'

'That too.'

'So what do you think?'

'About what?' I teased him.

'The clip,' he said, now irritated.

'You really want to know what I think?'

'Yes,' he said in a lowered voice, his breathing heavy.

'Really?'

'Just say it, Nitya.'

'You are a very crappy singer. Please avoid singing even in bathrooms,' I said and burst into laughter and quickly shut up when he didn't join me.

'Not funny. Just tell me your answer?'

'What answer?'

'Yes or no?'

'About what?'

'So you want to play games, huh? But remember one thing, this is my heart and not Sudoku. Still if you want to hear it from me then...' he said with a pause and I waited anxiously for the most magical words. My heart, my brain stopped.

'I love you and I want to spend the rest of my life with you,' he said.

My heart skipped a million beats. The earth stood still. The adrenaline rush I felt was unmatched. I had a zillion butterflies dancing in my stomach. I had never felt this way, not even when I completed all my exams for CA. I stayed silent as the feeling began to sink in.

'What's your answer?'

'I will think about it.'

'You have been speaking to me twenty hours a day for the last two months and still you want to think about it?' He asked amused. 'Strange.'

'Give me a week's time, at least.' I said and we chatted the night away. That night he told me that he loved me four more times. I could live with that for the rest of my life.

'BHAIYA, PLEASE PACK this mug,' I said taking out the wallet from my extra-large handbag. The mug read 'Thinking about you. You are special.'

I air-mailed it to San Francisco, from the address on his biodata, my first gift to him. A week later, I got a call from him.

'Switch on your cam,' Hitesh said.

'Now?' I asked in a deep baritone. I checked my watch. The clock showed 3 am.

'Yeah now.'

I plugged the cable and switched on my laptop. He was in his office kitchen, drinking coffee in the mug I had sent him.

'Don't you see something different?' he asked.

'Nice mug,' I smiled.

He kissed into the phone.

'Kiss? You phone-kissed me? You can't phone-kiss me. Woah not so soon, mister. You will have to pass through one thing before getting me.' I warned him even while I was half asleep.

'So now you are my girlfriend. Officially,' he said as if I were his possession.

'In your dreams,' I said. 'This is just a friendly gift.'

'So I am a special friend. The mug says so.'

'That you are.'

'WASSUP MY BITCHES?' Manav said as he stroked Malvika and my head simultaneously. He ignored the dirty looks we threw at him.

'Why was your phone busy yesterday?' Manav asked.

'Had a client meet on phone,' I lied. I couldn't tell them about Hitesh, not until things are official.

'Hmm…I see. Client meeting at two in the night?' Manav queried me like Sherlock Holmes.

'Why did you call me at two in the night by the way?' I counter-queried him to escape the interrogation.

'Answer my question first.'

'Because I was playing hard to get,' I tried to waive off the topic.

'How can you play hard to get when you are already hard to want?' said Manav laughing like a third grade villain.

'Today I think I am going to get my first assault charge,' I said as I stood up and pretended the TV remote to be my weapon. He pulled a nearby pillow as his bulletproof vest.

'And why were you awake till two?' Malvika asked him.

'I was talking to Yogeshwari.'

'Yogeshwari who?'

'This girl I met at the gym. You know she complimented me on my superman t-shirt which you crazy lot hate,' he said twitching his eyebrows victoriously.

'So what?' I asked bored.

'So? You still didn't get it?' He asked.

Malivika and I looked at each other, confused. It was as if the teacher had asked us the difference between mitosis and meiosis.

'When a girl compliments a guy, it means that she wants to have sex with him, you dumbos!'

Malvika and I entered a fit of laughter.

'This is what guys think? Really?' I asked surprised at his naivety.

'Of course. Ask that *Jungli Balli,*' Manav said, a little offended. *Jungli Balli* a.k.a Balwinder, was one of the gym instructors at the Gold's gym who gave bro tips to Manav.

'Or maybe it's your new deodorant which makes you a sex magnet,' I said in a very serious tone.

'She liked three pictures of mine on Facebook.'

'You sent her a friend request also? You are fast.'

'Clearly she wants to sleep with you,' I slapped my palm on his back and let him continue with his fantasy. His heart was going to break soon.

'BHAVIN KNOWS, TEJAS knows, Viren knows, my colleague Mandy knows... my di knows... everyone around me knows about us. Name one friend of yours who knows about us. Do Malvika, Komal or Manav know about this? Did you tell your Monali bhabhi?' He said fuming. This was our third fight in a week on the same topic. 'Forget it. You have not even told me.'

Having exhausted my high-speed internet usage quota for the month in one week on our Skype sessions, I called directly on his mobile. Eleven rupees per minute. Life seemed a bitch.

'Hitesh, I will tell you when I feel it. Not like this, forcefully, ok? And second thing, I don't need to tell ten people about us to give you the assurance of our relationship. We are not even committed. Things are not finalised. I can't go about beating drums about something which is not even confirmed. What if there are some issues later? You know how our society is.'

'You don't trust me, do you? You care for the whole fucking society, but not me,' he was hurt.

'I trust you more than anyone else,' I mellowed, 'and that is why we are talking since four months and I haven't even met you.

Besides, I have told my mom about us. I went one step ahead and told my mom. She knows that I am very interested in you. Isn't that enough? Isn't that more than telling your friends?'

'I don't know what to say,' he was not convinced.

'Listen Hitesh, I see my future with you. Don't let these minor issues come between us, please. And quite frankly, I am bored of this subject. I like you and that is why I have stopped meeting other guys. Now let's talk about something else, please,' I said.

We remained silent for five minutes which seemed like five hours, waiting for either to kill ego and speak first.

'What happened to your tickets? Did you speak to your agent?' I finally broke the ice.

'Getting cancelled,' he replied sadly.

'I knew it. I knew it,' I said utterly disappointed. Such a crappy day.

'Hey, don't be so upset. I will see you in December. I can't come there without my visa being stamped or I will risk my future with this company. Our future,' he said. Inwardly I thanked God that we moved to some other topic and for a change it was him who was convincing me.

Tables had turned.

'I understand but I was so excited about it. I have been waiting for you for months.' My mood was off.

'So am I, baby,' he said. 'It's just a matter of a few more months.'

'My mom and relatives are pressurizing me to keep meeting other guys. What should I tell them?'

'So what, yaar? Meet them and then refuse. Say you don't like them. Make any excuse. *Arey*, I will give you some very good reasons. Now cheer up, my honey. I hate your upset tone. One more thing, my sister wants to speak to you. Let's con call this weekend.'

'Yeah sure,' I said as he tried to distract me. Talking with his sister, it was an assurance that he was serious about our relationship and wanted to take it to the next level by involving our family members. I was relieved.

'What's your goal weight, *Golu*?' Hitesh said tongue-in-cheek.

'Hey don't call me Golu...you...you....Mr America!' I threatened him with my tweezers on our Skype video chat.

'You know what my di told me yesterday? Settle for a girl who has a sexy body like Vishali. Boy, she is really hot. Check her out on my friend list. She is so gorgeous,' he said. I got a third degree burn.

Why would some people think that gaining attention from other women would want to make their girlfriends want them even more? I hated that Vishali. I hated his sister and I hated him. Insecurity is such a comic emotion to watch.

'Why would I check her out? I am straight,' I replied off-handedly as I did a post-mortem of her profile. *Let's see what she has got that I don't.*

A girl wearing shorts in high heels appeared on my screen as I scanned her photo after photo. Pouting, winking, dancing, eating cupcakes, making circles from hukka smoke. Ok got it. She was really tall and did not have even one inch of extra fat on her body. She tied her hair in a puff higher than Mount Kilimanjaro. Her face was very average but I guess none of the guys felt the need to see it.

'Aww you got jealous. Ha ha I was just kidding,' he enjoyed watching me.

'Not funny.'

'Baby, you are my one and only sin theta and I am your cos theta, always,' he was gentling.

'Yeah and I don't want any kind of uncalled tangent in our trigonometry. Mind it!' I warned.

My medulla oblongata started a rivalry with the sexy force called Vishali. I resolved. *Before he comes to India for our wedding, I am getting in shape.*

'I have been thinking about our wedding....' I said with a little hesitation.

'Me too...' he said and smiled in the video.

'Really?' My eyes lit up, 'You too think about our wedding?'

'Think? I day-dream about it. How about a destination wedding? Somewhere in Bangkok?'

*Well that might just remain a day-dream unless you are going to sponsor it.*

'What?' I said a little shocked, 'My relatives would love it though, expenses carried out by me, of course.'

'Imagine you and me taking *pheras* on the beach,' he said romantically.

'Yeah, but that is for hi-fi parties. Maybe we can settle for a honeymoon there if you wish,' I said reasonably.

'Then what fits into your budget? A simple non-AC hall?' The tone of his voice switched from romantic to sarcastic in a nano-second.

It was a hard hit. Someone just showed me my status on my face. And that someone meant the world to me. The first thing I wanted to do was to switch off the webcam.

'I mean, see I am from the US and the youngest in the family. My parents have a huge social circle in India. So there are expectations from my relatives and all. I can't do anything under my status,' he gave an explanation.

'But there was no need to say what fits into your budget. You could have said it in a better way.' I said in a hurtful tone, fighting hard to control the disappointment in my voice.

'Ok look. I am sorry. I didn't mean it like that,' he pinched his ears to apologize. He looked so cute and innocent. My heart melted. 'We get married just once; I want to make it grand.'

'Is your grand destination wedding non-negotiable? We can divide the wedding expense if you wish.'

'But wedding is from the girl's side. Reception is from the groom's side. My parents would not agree with dividing the wedding expense thing.'

I remained silent.

'Would a wedding in a five-star hotel suit you?' he asked. He sounded like a salesman who would pitch you for Audi if you can't afford Ferrari.

'Umm... well... I will have to work on that,' I said, not promising him anything. Not yet.

ABOUT TEN TABS were opened on the bottom screen as I browsed through various halls and banquets for wedding venues. Imagine I was searching for my own wedding venue. I asked for the rates in Holiday Inn. Hitesh wanted a big memorable wedding. I wrote my wedding budget three times again from scratch.

'Madam, minimum two hundred people and the venue is free. We have up to five different costs per plate, ranging from fifteen hundred rupees to three thousand.'

I noted down all the information and calculated. Hitesh said that there were seven hundred to eight hundred people alone in their circle of family and friends. So if I cut down my group of people to fifty, then also I will be able to accommodate only five hundred of their people. I will just invite my immediate relatives. I was worked up the whole evening. I did the math and decided to take a loan for the wedding. I had some savings in ICICI and a couple of fixed deposits in SBI. That wouldn't have been enough. I nervously placed a hand over my head.

'Take the hand off. Goddess Laxmi won't bless us otherwise,' my mom said jerking off my hand and placing a cup of chai next to my computer.

'Right now, I need her help more than anyone'

'Do we really need this lavish a wedding?' My mom was concerned.

'Mom, this is the only thing he wants. I am just checking. Let's get an estimate first. We can cut back on functions like sangeet, engagement and grahshanti. Those will be simple.'

'What? You are cancelling Grahshanti also? No, not Grahshanti. That is mandatory.' My mom made a face.

I stayed silent. She took away the plate of khakhras which I had eaten earlier and then went to take her diabetes medicine. I felt really bad. To be honest, I wanted the sangeet function more than anything else. Mom saw my face and said, 'Actually you are right. What is the need of Grahshanti? Why to feed people we don't like double-double? And don't worry about money. I have your grandmother's jewellery which is out of fashion. We can sell those and get good money.' My heart melted at her sacrifice. 'We will have just one function. Wedding,' she added.

'Thanks mom but we are not selling anything,' that was all I could manage, mentally thinking where I could arrange extra money from or what else could I cut down on for including Grahshanti Puja.

'MAY I COME in, sir?' I knocked on Rudra's door though it was open. There is no harm in being extra courteous when you are going to speak to your boss about a pay raise.

'You may,' he said.

He looked up through his lashes and nodded at my presence. Strong smell of musk filled my nostrils as I walked in. Men and musk is a deadly mix. He looked jaw-dropping handsome in a plain brown shirt, total drool-worthy. *The colour suits him. In fact all colours suit him.*

*God! What am I doing? I am in a relationship with Hitesh. Does that mean that I can't even appreciate any other man even in my thoughts?*

'Nitya?' He said my name a little louder this time. 'Tell me.'

'Sir, I want an increment,' I said and stood still. I had forgotten all my planned tactics and strategy to manipulate him into increasing my salary.

He stared at me like a computer crash.

*Be strong, you king kong. Be strong, you king kong.* I kept chanting this motivating mantra to myself in my head.

'What?' He tilted his head, his voice dangerously low. 'You want what?' He asked me like I was asking for a piece from his ancestral property. I knew he had heard it the first time.

*Pay raise. Pay raise.*

'Sir, I have something very important coming up. I need a hike.' I said stressing the word 'hike'.

'You will have to wait till March next year when ratings are out,' he said looking straight into my eyes. I should have been angry but I flushed. I adjusted a stray lock of hair behind my ear. *His presence makes me so self-conscious. Why are Pooja and Jhanvi so smitten by him?*

'Send Ajay into my cabin,' he dismissed me.

If you want something badly enough, you don't stop for anyone or anything until you get it. I will apply for a loan.

I gave a brief description of my meeting with Rudra to Ajay.

'*Aak thoo,*' Ajay mock-spitted. '*Tumhe kya laga?Sardar khush hoga?*Increment *dega?*' I ignored his filmy comment.

'How long does it take for the loan money to be transferred to your account?' I asked him tapping my long fingernails anxiously on the kitchen counter. A cockroach ran back into microwave hiding.

'Two working days max. Why?'

'No. Just asking for information.' I dismissed his interrogation. 'And what is the maximum amount you can borrow?'

'Up to three times your current salary.'

'Ahan.' I made a mental record of his every word, 'and instalment?'

'About ten to fifteen percent of your monthly salary.'

'I can explain you more over dinner tonight,' Ajay said blushing.

I was taken by surprise. I always had my doubts that he liked me, but today he was making it a little more explicit.

'No, that's quite alright. I have got all the information I need to know and besides I don't want to keep you from anything.' I turned to go.

'No really. I am free. And I can also give you more details on other banks you can apply to which offer better interest rates and give you a brief on the paperwork too.' He was bribing me like a stranger offering sweets to a five-year-old.

I agreed. Hitesh is not going to like this.

'Thanks ya... you are such a good friend.' I smiled and friend-zoned him instantly. He smiled with satisfaction. Maybe he did not understand.

I will have to keep this meeting formal. Very formal.

I SPOTTED HITESH'S sister from a distance. She looked exactly like him, just a female version, and a little on the wheatish side. She wore knee-length denims with a dark pink sleeveless top.

'Hi... Nima di... right?' I said. It was so different meeting her in person. I had heard so much about her. Looking at her face was difficult and odd.

'Hi... How are you?' She took my hand in hers. 'How was your journey?'

'It was alright,' I replied smiling.

'Mom, this is Hitesh's sister, Nima di,' I said. I was calling her *di* all the while to make her believe that I have already accepted her as my elder sister.

They both greeted each other as we made our way towards their car. The plan was that both the families will meet for lunch in a restaurant and thereafter me and mom would visit Siddhivinayak and then board our train just in time.

'She is also dark?' Mom made a cutting remark as we lagged behind. Thankfully, it out of the hearing range of Nima di. I widened my eyes and lip synced, 'Keep quiet.'

His parents were already in the car waiting for us. His father occupied the front seat and his mother the passenger seat. Nima di took the driving seat and I sat in the middle between two moms, which briefly reminded me of my meeting with Jig-ness's parents.

'Jai Shri Krishna,' my mom folded her hands.

'Jai Shri Krishna,' both his parents responded in unison.

'Came properly no? Any difficulty?' His mommy asked as if she had made the arrangements for our travel.

No we are still in train, would be my usual response, but I decided to keep the sarcasm to myself. These days my sarcasm had reached a level where even I didn't know if I am joking or saying something genuinely.

'No, no aunty. Pleasant journey,' I said as politely as I could. If she were to be my future mother-in-law, I couldn't afford to displease her in any way. She was his mom, 'the'mom.

'This Mumbai heat and traffic *na*, I hate it. But at least it's better than Dubai,' his sister cursed the long fleet of beeping cars.

'*Arey* yes beta, you are from Dubai *na*? Where do you stay? I have some relatives staying in Bur Dubai,' my mom asked.

'Aunty I stay in Karama which is very close to Bur Dubai,' she answered looking in the rear-view mirror. This is the thing about Dubai. More than celeb-spotting, it has nowadays become a place for relative spotting.

WE ARRIVED AT a restaurant where they served Gujarati Thalis – fixed meal. His father began the conversation as the waiters served the starters one-by-one.

'So have you studied the *Bhagvad Gita*?' My future father-in-law asked me after few formal questions.

'Yes uncle, I have,' I replied.

'Ok, so tell me, what did Krishna say to Arjun between the war?'

'That one should perform his duties even if his own brother is standing in front of him,' I gave a short and straightforward answer.

'Yes, but what exactly did he say?' He pressed for more information.

He asked me if I had studied the *Bhagvad Gita,* but I had only read it. I was lost for words as he took my interview.

'Ok, I will ask you an easy one. Recite the fifth *shlok* or explain what does it say?'

'Fifth *shlok*? Yeah fifth *shlok*...' I pretended to remember as I took a sip of water to buy some time to think something clever.

'It says that one should perform his duties without worrying about the fruit,' I said the only thing I knew about *Mahabharata*.

'Wrong,' he tapped the table. The steel glasses shook. 'It says that all is rooted in time, to be or not to be, to be happy or not to be happy.'

Clearly, my answer had made him root in unhappiness.

'Oh yes, yes, yes, I remember I remember,' I lied. 'Uncle, must say you have immense knowledge about religion,' I buttered him. He smiled proudly like he had written the *Bhagvad Gita* himself. If nothing works, pay compliments, that gives the ego a good massage.

'So beta, you have never stayed in a joint family?' It was his mother's turn now.

'I have many cousins aunty, but I have never stayed in a joint family,' I said. Her face turned sour. I was hoping it would be from the buttermilk.

'We have always stayed in a joint family. And our extended family gathers on holidays at our farmhouse in our village and we play cards all night long,' Nima didi said only from the memory of joy that joint family brings.

'I always wanted a big family. I don't have any siblings so I missed out all the fun while growing up,' I replied so that I can be thought of as a person who wants to adjust and accept people.

'There is lot of work also, but everyone helps each other,' she said.

'Why? You don't have a maid?' My mom asked her.

'No. We don't believe in maids. They don't clean as good as we do. Only us women can take care of our house.'

Having a maid is a pre-requisite for a groom. Though there is division of labour in the family, it can't be substituted for not having a maid. My mom's face fell a little.

'So when is Hitesh planning to come to India?' My mom asked next.

'Next January. He was going to come in April but due to visa issues, he had to postpone his plan,' his father said.

We discussed some more about my education, career, his education, his career, some embarrassing stories of his childhood which was my favourite part. I must say he has an amazing family.

They were really sweet and I would be more than lucky to be a part of it.

When the bill arrived, both me and Nima di pounced on the folder. Both of us insisted to pay the bill which left the paper in shreds. We asked for a new bill and then my mom and I allowed them to pay reluctantly.

While on our way back home, mom couldn't stop obsessing over how good those people were. They were radiating such positive energy, they would have been protons in past birth. When we crossed the Tapi river, I just said a small prayer and threw a coin in the water. I tried to call Hitesh but the network was unavailable. *Did his family like me? Will they accept me?* A thousand questions were running through my mind. I was getting an anxiety attack. Thoughts of meeting his extended family kept coming back to me.

WE REACHED HOME at midnight. It would be noon in the US. I called Hitesh to give him the good news. I was so excited that I ditched Skype and phoned his mobile directly.

'Hey beautiful…' He answered.

'Hiii…' I replied with the biggest 'hi' in the world with the biggest smile on my face.

'So how did it go?'

'Take a guess?'

'Just tell me yaar, excitement is killing me.'

'Hitesh, you have the most amazing parents ever. I loved them. My mom loved them.'

'Really?' He almost screamed out of joy but soon lowered his voice when he realized that he was still in office. 'You did?'

'They are the best. Did you speak to them? What did they say about me? Did they like me?' I shot questions at him.

'I don't know. I tried but it was not reachable. They must have slept. I will speak to them tomorrow morning.'

'And call me as soon as you have a word,' I added.

I couldn't sleep the whole night. This will be a fitting answer to Pappu mama and Jaina maasi and our neighbour Shaila aunty and everyone. It's finally happening. I am getting married. I tossed and turned and dreamt of playing *teen-patti* with his family.

'What happened? Did you speak to them?' I asked him the next morning as I made my coffee in the office.

'No my gorgeous, it's still unreachable. But don't worry. Who wouldn't love you? You are total lovable material Miss Nitya Trivedi, soon to be Mrs Nitya Hitesh Joshi,' he said.

'Ok, but Miss Nitya Trivedi is busy. But if you hear anything from them, just let me know. Gotta go.'

I came home from work and still hadn't received Hitesh's call. I was worried. I texted him asking if everything was alright? I didn't receive any reply from him. When you don't hear from the person you care about the most, all things negative start creeping into the mind.

'What happened? What did they say about you?' My mom asked me expectantly.

'Hitesh hasn't been able to speak to them yet.'

'Arey everything must be alright. I am going to offer five coconuts to Kshtrepal Bhagwan once things are finalised. Don't worry. It's definitely a yes from them. My heart says so,' she said.

I kept my fingers crossed.

I RECEIVED JUST one text from him in the next four days. He was in LA with his friends over the long weekend.

I checked the time zone on my mobile display and called him on Monday morning from my office. It must not be very late there.

He must be cooking dinner. My call was received on the sixth ring when it was about to go on voicemail.

'Hello,' he said a little silently.

'Oh thank god! Are you alright?' I said taking a deep breath.

'Yeah,' he replied.

'Where were you?' I asked concerned. 'You know I had all these scary thoughts when you didn't pick up my calls.'

'I was in LA with my friends.'

'Ahan,' I replied and we both fell silent.

'How are you?' He spoke after a few minutes.

Then it started to dawn that something was wrong. I thought of the worst – his parents disliked me.

'Not fine because something has happened and I don't understand what. You didn't tell me what your parents said,' I asked.

This is the thing about long-distance relationships. If you don't see people every day or every week, you don't know if they are starting to change. Phone calls and Skype sessions aren't same as spending actual in-person time with someone.

'Well, they said that she is a good girl but...' his voice began to trail off, 'but let's cool off the matter for now. They want to keep looking for more prospects,' he replied.

'But why?' I asked upset.

'Kundlis don't match,' he gave a very short answer.

'What crap! You matched the kundlis long back. You knew we are seven gunas short of the minimum required for a match, right? Then why the hell did you talk to me for four months?' I raised my voice. I didn't care about the glances I got from my colleagues.

'Look, I am sorry. My parents don't feel that you will be able to adjust in my big family,' he tried to explain.

'Hitesh, even my mom was not a big fan of yours. I convinced her, because I am serious about you. Why can't you do the same dammit?' I rose up from my chair making my way towards the main door. 'And besides, I never said that I don't like big families. What gave them that impression?'

'I don't want to spoil your future, Nitya. Just start looking for other guys. You are a great girl. You can get anyone you like.' He cited the most scripted lines.

'If everything boils down to family approval, then you had no right to talk to me for four months the way you did.' I fumed. 'You could have told me this thing four days back. I was waiting like crazy. My mom was waiting,' I wailed.

'I was with my friends in LA for a friend's birthday and I didn't want to spoil their mood because of me. So I waited for four days.'

'Can you believe your own words, Hitesh? I prayed to God for your safety while you were boozing away. You didn't for once think about me. This is how you set your priorities?' I went hysteric.

'I am sorry.'

'Sorry? You want to be forgiven? Ok then do one thing. Just apologize to my mom. Speak directly to her and tell her why you did this to me. Why you did this to her? If she forgives you, then I will also forgive you.'

'No. I won't do that.'

'Why not? You are answerable to her. Even I have my parents just as you.'

'Nitya please, you are my angel and I will always love you,' he mellowed his voice.

'Oh just shut the fuck up. I thank my stars that I didn't marry an asshole like you,' I said switching off the phone. I never use cuss words, this was the first time in my life.

I rushed to the bathroom and splashed cold water on my face. On way back to my desk, I got apologetic glances from everyone. Thankfully, Rudra was on leave, which is rare.

At about 6 pm, I packed my things and left.

My mom opened the door after two doorbells. I threw my handbag limply on the couch. She came after me, worried.

'What happened? Why your eyes are red? Did your manager say anything?'

'Did Hitesh say anything? I will speak to him,' she said pressing her hand on my forehead.

'He is not going to call me anymore. His parents did not like me.' I slumped beside my handbag, dabbing my fingers in my cornea to wipe off the emerging baby tears.

'What? Why?' she asked, her voice shocked. 'But they were so good to us that day.'

'Kundlis don't match…that is what he has to say. I don't know. They said that I won't be able to adjust in their joint family. I don't know,' I said as I blew nose in my *dupatta*.

'Wait, let me call his parents. I will settle everything,' my mom offered. Her voice was frail and nervous.

'No mom. You are not going to call him or anyone. If he doesn't have the guts to convince his parents, then why should you?' I said, 'It's over'.

I CHECKED MY email the next day. I had one unread email from Hitesh Joshi. My heart started racing. *Maybe he spoke to his parents about us.*

*Hi Nitya,*

*I know you will not talk to me and you should not.*

*Reasons?*

1. *I am a loser yaar.*

2. *I completely agree with you yaar that if I had to go with my family's choice, then I shouldn't have talked to you the way I did. And you are right that if my family had to select a bride for me, I shouldn't have stretched our relationship.*

3. *Whenever it comes to family, I get confused and I don't behave well with you like a good boyfriend should behave and the way good boyfriend should take care of his girlfriend as well which suggests that I can leave you any moment and that's well proven.*

*If I would be in your place, I would never talk to such a person.*

*Reasons why I am writing to you are:*

1. *It's not all about family and it's not because of my family that I suddenly started behaving different. I just got a spark of thought that if our relationship didn't work out, then what you will do and what I will do.*

   *It's a tough job for me. On one side, I love you and on the other side. I also have to think practically.*

2. *Other day I was talking to my sister about you for hours and hours and explaining to her how beautiful you are as a person too. Personally, I haven't ever seen such a pure hearted and innocent person in my life. But what scares me now is – what if I can't justify your feelings. You are a princess and you really deserve the best. Believe me, your love, your care, your thoughts, your attachment are all high up and they just don't deserve what you are getting from me.*

3. *I am not worried about myself if this love story doesn't work; I am just worried and concerned about you. I will regret if I won't be able to stand by you or I won't be able to justify your feelings.*

*I know these words don't matter anymore. I shouldn't even tell you that I love you. All that sounds stupid when it comes from me.*

*Only things I would like to convince you about:*

1. *We still haven't said 'NO'. But in case we do, then I don't want you to hold on. I am not trying to be diplomatic, nor am I giving you any explanations. I am also hurt, I can't see you crying. I can't hurt you. I am so worried yaar.*

   *I know it's not possible for you to talk to other boys immediately after what has just happened, but you are one in a billion. I understand everything. But please yaar, keep seeing other guys. I am a loser and I don't want to hold you back.*

2. *I really loved you and still do, but I don't know what to do.*

3. *It might sound selfish but* WILL YOU WAIT FOR ME TILL DECEMBER AND THEN WE WILL DECIDE TO PROCEED FURTHER OR NOT?

*I know it will take time for you to come to terms with this, but I hope you will be okay at the end and you will find your prince.*

*I will never forget our chats, talks and all. You gave me beautiful feelings. You are the first girl who gave me such nice feelings and though I might have flirted with hundreds of other girls, you were my first love.*

*I just don't want to hurt you, I just don't want to make you cry, and in some situations I just don't know what to do. The best way to not hurt the person in such a situation is to go away and that's what I am trying to do.*

*I wanna write a lot. What do I say? Don't cry yaar. You haven't lost anything. The only person to cry should be me and not you. You are a sweetheart.*

*You will never know how what I will lose in going with my family and marrying a girl of their choice. My heart will cry every day but I will do it for them and you will never know how much pain I will be through.*

*Anyway, I hurt you like hell. I behaved so badly, I deserve to be cursed. Yaar, you can talk to me anytime.*

*I would like to be your friend forever.*

*Please stay happy in life. What if we were together and you in even more misery after marriage. Good we broke up and now we are free.*

*Chal take care,*

*H-IT-ESH*

'STILL WE HAVEN'T said no', 'Wait for me till December' – I read this line three more times. I pulled down my laptop screen. I paced around the room impatiently. My father had told me that one should wait for at least twenty-four hours before reacting to a negative situation. I kept my cool and two days later, I gave a fitting reply to his essay.

> *Hitesh,*
>
> *Don't feel bad about yourself, because I don't hate you. I am indifferent. You have mistaken me for a girl who will wait for a guy who 'may' or 'may-not' marry her. Oh I am also not buying your kundli excuse, because you had matched our kundlis long back (refer point four from your first email). In this one day's time I have realised that this break up is one of the best things that has happened to me. Who I marry is not your concern, you worry about yours.*
>
> *'Still we haven't said no'...Hitesh, I am saying no and this time it is for keeps. I was waiting for my knight in shining armour and all I got in you was a loser wrapped in aluminium foil. See you wanted me to move on, and I am moving on. So let me.*

I PRESSED SENT and signed off. That night I cried myself to sleep, again.

Next day in office was terrible. I hadn't eaten anything since morning. I didn't want to sit at home because that would drive me crazier. I needed distraction. I wore my glasses and tied my hair up in a bun wearing the dullest *kurti* I could lay my hands on. I arrived before anyone, and fortunately my boss, Rudra noticed that.

He wore a crisp sky-blue shirt, sleeves rolled to his elbow.

'Why Miss Nitya...early today?' He wished me morning.

'Yes sir, I woke up early,' I said keeping my glance low. I felt like I would start crying any minute even if I made the slightest eye contact with anyone.

'Good. You have set an example for other employees,' he appreciated. I nodded, my eyes still downcast.

'Are you ok?' He suddenly asked, his voice concerned.

'I am fine,' I replied.

'You sure?' He tormented me with confirmation questions.

*What's his problem? Why can't he leave me alone?*

'Ahan,' I nodded switching on my computer.

'Did anyone say anything to you?'

'No, no. I am good. Blocked nose and runny eyes,' I said.

'There is something else,' he said.

He stood rooted to the spot making it really hard to believe in 'this too shall pass'.

Tear gas. Shit! I should have said that cops sprayed tear gas over a silent protest in my area and I was caught up in that. Seeing the country's current unrest, he would have believed me.

I started typing furiously. He eyed me for a long minute and left when I didn't respond. I audited, re-audited, checked all the files I could. All the employees went past asking if I was ok. I just answered in monosyllables. I skipped my coffees and lunch. And then Hitesh called me. I didn't receive his call. He called me again. I put the phone to silent. He called again. I saw the light blinking, lay the phone face down and rushed to the bathroom. I splashed water on my face.

'What happened? Are you crying?' Jhanvi knocked the door.

'No. Nothing. I am fine.' I told strongly. I hoped she wouldn't call Pooja.

'Sure?' She insisted. *Why is everyone asking me 'are you sure?'*

'Yeah,' I said. I just wanted to be left alone. I returned to my desk and started typing violently. The keyboard could have broken any minute.

On his fifth call, I picked up.

'Hello,' I said. My heart pounded. I was going to hear his voice after four long torturous days. *Did he call to reconcile?* A hope sparked in me.

'Hi,' he said and became silent. 'You didn't pick up my phone?'

In a relationship when you think that you are over someone, why does that one 'hi' from that person make your mighty resolutions shake.

'I was busy,' I answered quickly.

'Why are you acting this way? Are you ok?' He asked in a worried tone.

*Acting this way?* A part of me wanted to react like hydrochloric acid.

'I am fine. What would happen to me?' I said carelessly but not too carelessly so that he wouldn't ask me again. I wanted this conversation to happen.

'Ok then, bye. I don't have all day,' he sounded unconcerned. I just shut the phone.

I looked up towards the ceiling so that the tears don't fall free on my face. At that time, Rudra walked up to me.

'Nitya, you seem unwell,' he said, 'you can leave soon if you like'.

All employees began to notice for he had spoken the words he had never said before. He asked me to take half day leave.

'No sir, I am fine. Just a little cold.' I sniffed noisily into my tissue. All the colleagues by this time were giving me looks that indicated I must be mad to reject his offer.

'Go home.' Rudra said in a stern voice, 'Come back on Monday'. All eyes looked at him in disbelief.

'Your work will not be productive if you are ill, anyway,' he made a suggestive excuse. Pooja and Jhanvi looked at him opened-mouthed.

'Thank you,' I switched off the computer and grabbed my bag because I didn't want to create a scene anymore. Half day of entertainment was enough.

I LAY IN my bed in the dark when the door-bell rang three to four times in succession. I knew it was the girls. Only they had the nerves to do this and get away un-abused by my mom. I hadn't touched my laptop in four days.

'Mom, please don't switch on the lights. It's hurting my eyes.' I pulled the sheets on my face as she opened the door.

'Look who has come,' she said nudging my feet.

'Now you both only speak to her,' she said to Komal and Malvika in a worried voice. 'She has been like this for the last four days'.

'Don't worry aunty, we are here.' Malvika took over like a trained doctor as mom closed the door behind her.

I squirmed as she pulled the sheets from my face. I saw fireflies everywhere. I placed my elbow on my eyes as my eyes adjusted to the brightness.

'First you didn't receive our phone calls and then... oh God!' she changed the topic midway, 'Look at your dark circles. You look like a panda.' She looked at me like I was a mental-at-large.

'You are stinking, eww.' Komal pinched her nose, 'go and take a shower. We are going out.'

'No *yaar*. We will order a takeaway,' I resisted as I tied my unruly hair into a bun.

'Miss Nitya, take a shower now.' Malvika threatened me like I was an errant child, 'or we will have to give you a bath. And it will be very embarrassing for all three of us then, isn't it Komal?'

'Baby, you know how much I love truth and dare. I will do it,' Komal warned.

I jumped to my feet almost instantly and ran to the bathroom grabbing whatever clothes I could from my wardrobe.

'You have ten minutes,' she shouted as she increased the volume of a latest Bollywood item number on her phone.

I felt good as I poured cold water over me. It was painful at first but after a couple of rounds, you get used to it eventually. Only if forgetting some people was as easy as that. I scrubbed myself till I was squeaky clean and fifteen minutes later we were on our way to Maheshwari to eat my favourite Pav bhaji, triple seat on Komal's Activa.

'TWO PAV BHAJIS and one mysore masala dosa.' Komal ordered for all three of us – 'everything in butter'. Don't we just love people who don't even have to look at the menu for placing an order. It was the Maheshwari Food Centre. Not the most happening food joint, but definitely the best in taste.

It was a Thursday night and thankfully not a very busy night. Komal selected a corner seat for us so we could keep the public attention to minimum if I chose to grieve.

We didn't speak for five minutes. I buried my head in the mobile to avoid their sharp are-you-going-to-say-something-or-not glances. I switched on my mobile after four days. I had one hundred and thirty one emails, half of them spam and not one from Hitesh. They eyed each other as to which one of them was going to ask me first.

'You have hurt us a lot,' Malvika finally said, snatching the phone away from me. 'You went through so much and didn't even say a single thing to us'.

'What do I say?' I said trying to hold a choke, 'that a girl like me who gave relationship advice to all needs to console herself?'

'Someone who considered other people's heartbreak as boredom had her own heart broken by a loser,' I said

'What? You think I am a bore?' Komal said disbelievingly, 'Malvika, did you hear what she said'? Komal always counted on me whenever she fought with her boyfriend Arjun.

'Err... umm... actually what she said is correct,' Malvika said daring to look at Komal. 'No offence to you though.'

'Hmm...none taken,' Komal said as she realized that it was about me and not her that day. 'What was his name by the way?'

'Hitesh Joshi.' I said meekly, hating to speak his name.

'Oh wait,' Malvika said as she fished for her phone, 'is this the guy?' She showed me his photo on Facebook.

'Yes. But how do you know?' I asked

'Show, show,' Komal craned her neck into her phone.

'When you added him and we had no mutual friends, I just got curious, you know,' Malvika explained.

'You liked him? Over all the handsome guys you can get, him? Really? He is so dark. How are you going to find him at night?' Komal laughed and high-fived Malvika. And from there the guy-bashing started. I felt good. They said just the things that I wanted to hear.

'Actually his sister who is considered the fairest of them all is still darker than my darkest cousin Premal.' I discriminated him on his skin colour. I was being very cheap, I know, but trust me, I felt better. Once you hate someone, everything they do or don't do is offensive. For example, 'Look at that bitch drinking water like she owns the place'.

Komal and Malvika laughed wildly to encourage me to humiliate him more and I must say that they were faring well. At least that made me laugh and, trust me, it's way better than crying on pillows.

'And what is with his teeth? Such bright colour doesn't go well with his skin tone,' Malvika said this time. 'No need for electricity.

Just tell him to smile during a power failure and it will work as a charged battery. Imagine how much money you could save'.

'And environment friendly too,' Komal added.

We laughed so hard, took a moment to breathe and laughed again.

'Good one,' I said. I was supposed to cry and here I was laughing till I cried.

This was getting so much better than I thought. In my mind I thanked the girls and my mom a million times for dropping by.

The waiter placed the smoking hot Pav bhaji in front of us. I didn't realize I was so hungry. I dug in right away and before the waiter left the table, I ordered some extra Pav too.

'Now I realize. Once he told me that he was going to deposit a thousand dollars in my account but he never did,' I said finger licking the Pav bhaji. 'Not that I wanted his money, but he was speaking crap. *Kuch bhi kuch bhi.*'

'Then he said that he has bought three iPhones, latest versions, the ones with Facetime. One for his sister, one for his mother and one for me,' I added, 'and he was persistently asking for my home address so he can deliver'.

'You should have taken the mobile, yaar. Watch and learn from Komal. See, how she is using Arjun!' Malvika said at a glaring Komal.

'I denied because it was too early to accept gifts from him and you know what he said? If I had your address I would have sent it to you directly.' I shrugged. 'My address was everywhere'. I gave evidence. 'In the biodata I had sent him, on shaadi.com, like everywhere.'

'You should have pointed that out then,' Komal said. 'Take the phone and after the break up say that you can't return because it got stolen or something. Simple'.

'You think I didn't try?' I asked

'You did. But not hard enough…' Malvika said.

Malvika and Komal made a stupid pact like they would be the gatekeepers to not allow me to be anywhere near Hitesh or anything that remotely reminds me of him. Not that he was near me or anything but they deleted his number from my mobile, spammed his emails and blocked his Facebook page.

Our conversation was interrupted by Manav's phone call on Malvika's mobile. She went out to receive his call and came back after a couple of minutes.

'He wants to speak to you.' She handed me the phone.

'Sup? How you doin, baby?' Manav spoke from the other end. I gave a feeble smile into the phone.

'Hello to you too. Why aren't you here?'

'Cause I already knew that there is going to be a lot of guy-bashing.'

'Omniscient you are,' I said sipping some Pepsi.

'See listen, I don't know much about your sob story but I want to say just one thing. Most men are not like him, that I can guarantee. There are plenty out there who would treat you right. Just find one in a million other men who aren't afraid of love. And next time, be logical.' His tone became a little serious.

'Logical? But feelings are not supposed to be logical, right?' I said as he tried to restore my faith in men.

'Don't worry. You will bounce back. Keep the flow of your emotions in check, only for now.'

'It's my heart, not an air-conditioner. I cannot control its flow or temperature.'

'Ok then, just ask one question to yourself. Do you really want to be with someone who doesn't want you?'

Lightning struck my head. He was right. Why hasn't anyone put it this way to me before? Why would you want to be with someone who doesn't want to be with you! Simple.

'Do you really want to be with someone who doesn't want you back?' I repeated this question to myself several times in my head.

'Manav, you deserve a standing ovation. Enough said,' I was floored.

And just like that, I was over...over Hitesh (or so I thought). In five flat days to be precise. Not that I didn't hate him, but friends helped me cushion the blow. I was back in the matrimonial market.

# I Can't Stop Drinking About You

'Why is this background blurred?' Komal's mom blurted at Manav's photographic skills. 'Kuku get me my glasses,' she shrieked at one of the children running around.

'*Arey nai* aunty, this is how photos are clicked these days so it creates a 3D image. See how Rushabh's picture looks sharp with a natural smile,' Manav tilted his SLR camera and pointed a finger at the screen.

Komal had hired Manav as the professional photographer for her brother Rushabh's budget wedding. And Manav also wanted a break so he happily agreed to the offer. He was being paid peanuts, but since the past two years he was not able to get anywhere except making a Facebook page and begging his friends to press the 'Like' button.

'This is how you take pictures these days? Unclear pictures? You take proper pictures I am telling you or else I will take my advance back,' Komal's mom threatened a scared Manav, 'and not a single picture of the whole group?'

'But aunty I am a candid photographer. Traditional photographers capture groups, I take more informal, natural looking, in-the-moment kind of shots,' he spoke like a lamb trying to convince a tiger to spare him.

'I don't know all that. You do as I say. Don't go here and there. Stand in front of the stage and click everyone's photographs,' she said flashing her sari so bright pink in colour, it hurt my eyes. She walked away to bask in the five-star service provided by the bride's side.

Manav looked at Komal helplessly.

'Take my picture. But the background should be clear,' I mocked an upset Manav as I adjusted the safety pin on my shoulder.

Komal, the social ladder climber of our group could tell the year, make and model of any person within the first five seconds of meeting. When we were in the eighth standard, she had a major crush on one of our classmates, Arjun, who was also the only heir of one of the richest textile merchants of Surat. She knew that if she wanted to drive all those four by fours and convertibles then she had to convert this crush into love, quick and fast, before any other girl made her move.

So for this, first she started doing rounds of Arjun's place on the pretext of exchanging homework and class notes. No sooner, she had his mother and sister wrapped around her little finger. Then she saved some money by doing some odd jobs like babysitting to join the same tuition class as Arjun, knowing that this was going to be a worthy investment in the long term. Any other girl who came inches close to Arjun had to face Komal's wrath.

Once Komal saw Arjun's ex, Niharika, flirting with him. She walked up to her and lied, 'Oh you are the ex? I am the upgrade. Now get lost.'

With no girls near him, in at least fifty miles of radius, Arjun had no choice but to be with Komal as all his friends started having a girlfriend or two and he wanted to catch up. More than her beauty, Arjun was impressed by Komal's persistence.

Whenever they went out for a movie, Komal would pay for her ticket. Whenever they planned a dinner, they would split the bill. She was the kind of girl every guy dreamed of, the non-rip off kind. Komal would never leave a chance to show that she was not a gold digger and she loved him truly. She not only won his trust but also bagged his papaji, mummyji and sister. If their family had any internal feuds, they would call her to resolve. His mother would call her to check on Arjun if he had his lunch or not. His sister would ask for solutions to her problems in realtionships. For them, she was the daughter-in-law of their family already.

Three years later, because of Arjun's dad's powerful contacts and recommendations, Komal's father got the capital, land and clients for his chemical business. Her brother Rushabh worked under Arjun's dad's guidance in their diamond business as a junior and frequented Europe to deal with overseas clients, business class. The spare Honda City that Arjun's family reserved for guests was more or less found in Komal's parking lot. They were also able to move to a better flat in a posh area just after five years of Komal knowing Arjun. Komal now only kept contact with high profile people and slowly deleted people who were of no use to her. How Manav, Malvika and I survived in her friend-list is also a million-dollar question.

So when it came to Komal's brother's wedding, she kept him away from all the girls who were coming from middle class and had the potential to be a social ladder climber like her. The bride she found for him was no less in social status than Arjun. The girl's side arranged for a wedding in a five-star hotel with all high profile people attending it. They also had a leading Bollywood singer to perform at the wedding.

'Shhh...just follow me.' Malvika dragged me to a white four by four with tinted glass windows.

'What are you doing? Are you kidnapping me?' I asked.

'Shut up! You want me to gag you with my dupatta for the real feel?' she took long strides in her magenta lehenga.

She knocked on the window of the rear seat and Manav signalled us to get in quickly.

There were several empty and filled bottles of Jack Daniel's, Cobra, Kingfisher neatly placed in one of the cardboard boxes. Manav, Komal, Arjun and three other guys from the girl's family were already having shots.

'Guys…,' I said shocked but still kept my voice low, 'What are you up to?'

'Binge drinking,' Arjun giggled.

'You can't drink...it's…' I said

'Prohibited in Gujarat?' Manav interrupted, 'not anymore,' he said as he spread his arms to show me the exclusive range they had. 'Here. Take your pick.'

'For God's sake, there is a marriage going on out there,' I tried to reason.

'Marriage is over there, but the party is here, my darling.' Malvika said, 'Take this!'

'Yuck…don't bring it near me. I hate this smell. And who got this thing here?' I dabbed my orange duppata to my nose.

'The girl's side wanted to give a little treat to the privileged members of the family. Cheers.' Komal sounded a little tipsy already.

'But I have one complain guys,' Komal turned to the blokes of the girl's side, 'You started the shoe bid at five thousand rupees, five fucking thousand rupees. Not fair.'

'Yeah but you got your brother married in a five star… five fucking star,' Malvika imitated her tone.

'That's like even more than the amount you spent to trap Arjun, isn't it Komal?' Manav said, his voice intoxicated. 'Hey, but no worries. You will find many opportunities to redeem it. You always do.'

'Manav, shut up!' I said taking away his glass, before things got ugly.

'What? You trapped me? I thought you loved me.' Arjun held a choke, shocked by the revelation. No one paid him enough attention.

'Your mom says that I don't take good pictures. She told me that my pictures are blurry,' Maanav said to Komal hugging his camera. 'See Canon baby, see what this wretched world has to tell us. Even Galileo was not appreciated in his time.'

Malvika still tried to push the glass to my lips. I just shrugged off.

'Waiter, one vodka for me and water on the rocks, neat, for this lovely lady here.' Arjun placed the order to one of the blokes in the front seat.

'Why aren't you drinking? You are not underage *naa*? Because you look like one,' one of the bride's cousin asked.

'Short height to my advantage,' I smiled sarcastically.

'There are two types of people that annoy me. Drunk people when I am sober and sober people when I am drunk. So don't be so stuck up and have one.' Komal snatched the glass from Malvika and started thrusting it in my mouth, spilling alcohol all over my expensive lehenga.

'Drink. Drink. Drink. Drink,' others shouted in the background.

I managed to gulp down the whole thing in one shot. I felt a current down my body.

'Yay! Good girl gone bad,' Maanav and Arjun started clapping at my achievement.

'Eww…this tastes so bitter. Why would anyone enjoy this? And I don't even feel high.' I said very certainly.

'Hmm correct…you look pretty fine. Not bad for your first drink. This Tequila should do the trick.' Komal handed me a shot glass.

'No lemon? No salt?' I asked. 'You should have it with lemon and salt, I saw in movies.'

'Naah... just have it ya,' Malvika said popping a peanut in her mouth.

I downed it in one sip and felt a burning sensation down my throat.

I chuckled slowly. Then I chuckled a little louder and then I don't know what got into me that I started laughing loudly. It was enough to send a wave of uproar amongst my fellow drunkards.

'Cheers to Komal's brother Rushabh. Cheers to Komal and Arjun for true love, some wonderful years ahead. Woho.' I raised my empty glass. Everyone clinked to that.

'But there is nothing like true love you know...' I said feeling extremely light-headed, laughing to myself. Laughing at how life treated me. Komal and Arjun looked at each other uncomfortably.

'Well, here comes the emotions...' Manav palmed his face. Komal squeezed his thigh to shut him up.

And then suddenly I began to cry and I really didn't know why.

'Hey...why are you crying?' Manav sat beside me and gently rubbed my shoulders, 'See you have your eyeliner running all over your face'.

'No way. I am not crying. My mascara is way too expensive to be spent over a jerk like him,' I said pushing away the puddle of tears with my fist.

Manav held out Malvikas's duppatta for me. 'Here.'

She pulled it back in reflex. 'Designer piece, you know,' she said to me apologetically.

'Why? Is Sabyasachi your uncle? It's a duplicate stitched by Mangu Tailor specialist in ladies dress. Huh designer piece.' Manav rolled his eyes.

'And yes, cheers to the end of my relation-shit.' I spoke more to myself like others didn't exist.

'End of your toxic relation-shit,' Komal corrected.

I was still dismayed by the pain of being rejected. Dismayed by the feeling of being unimportant to someone, who was once the most important person to me.

'It's ok to screw up in a relationship. It's very much like screwing up in an examination. Life doesn't end there. You fail, you try again and then you pass and bounce back.'

'On the brighter side, see it as a lesson. Now you know what you want from a relationship,' Komal said.

'Now cheer up. It's totally his loss. Now buck up and show him that you are better without him,' Komal comforted me.

'Babe, you are going to get the best. Just wait and watch.' Malvika smiled at me.

'How do you know?' I looked hopefully at her like a baby.

'Call it sixth sense, intuition,' she replied, bringing balance to her mind.

Just then my phone rang.

'Hi, is this Nitya?' a male voice spoke from the other end.

'Speaking,' I tried to sound sober.

'Hi I am Abhishek. Today we had to meet at San Churro for a coffee?'

'Ermm.' I tried to recall. This liquor was making all my senses weak.

'For matrimonial,' he provided more information.

*Ring a bell?* Yeah Girish kaka from Singapore met this hi-profile investment banker sometime back and gave my number so we could meet during his visit to India.

'I am waiting at...,' the guy from the other end spoke.

'Yeah right, am on my way. Be there in five.' I hung up.

Matrimonial meeting after I was *peeke* tight. This is going to be fun.

'HI... I AM Abhishek and you must be Nitya?' A guy with a rare confidence extended his hand towards me.

'Hi, how do do?' I asked tipsy as I placed my hand in his. He looked at me, a little amused.

'Sorry, I mean how do you?' I managed to say in a drunken state. He kept silent and began to observe me.

'I mean how do you do? Sorry, my bad...my bad.' I raised my hand apologetically.

'Not too bad…please have a seat,' he pulled a chair for me.

'Aww that's so sweet of you, such a gentleman you are,' I said stopping the urge to tap his cheek. Booze makes you want to do crazy things.

'Thank you very much,' he smiled. 'Nice lehenga by the way.'

'Isn't it? Oh and just so you know that I am all decked up because I just came from Rushabh's wedding. Don't get any wrong impression,' I mock-warned him. I said widening my eyes to focus on him. His expression told me that I was acting really crazy. My head wouldn't stop spinning. I don't know why.

'Of course not,' he signalled the waiter to get the menu.

'So you are a chartered accountant?'

'Ahan.' I nodded. 'And you are?'

'An investment banker by *majboori* and a pianist by choice.'

'Oh no, not an investment banker. They are so boring.' I said folding my hand under my bust to express my disappointment. He started laughing.

'I hate them too but you know things we have to do for a living,' he said taking the menu from the waiter who looked at me and placed two fingers at his nostril like something was stinking. I sniffed myself but my sense of smell would not co-operate.

'Strawberry thick shake for me and a lemonade for madam,' Abhishek said without even asking me.

'You didn't even ask me. Rude. Rude. Rude.' I held my head to stop it from spinning.

'You will have lemonade,' he summoned. 'Please bring some extra lemon and salt.' He dismissed the waiter.

'Yeah, lemonade on the rocks would be great, with that fancy umbrella.' I smiled cheekily.

He pulled out a pack of cigarette and offered me. I shook my head in denial.

'Smoking is injurious to health. Read.' I took the packet from his hand and showed him the bold instructions, 'See.'

'*Achha*? Even boozing is injurious to health,' he said as he popped a cigarette in his mouth.

'What? You drink alcohol too?' I asked him all surprised. He grinned.

'Hmm...sometimes. And you?' he queried leaving a trail of laughter.

'Never.' I shook my head from the alcohol effect.

'Of course you don't,' he said as he took a drag. I waited for the smoke to clear so that I could have a good look at him. He was casually dressed in a dull grey Superdry t-shirt and white Converse. Someone had decided to look pretty rich for casuals too. Two small dimples made craters on his cheeks whenever he smiled. He looked intelligent, like the guy who could surely manage to win at least fifty lakhs in *KBC*.

We kept silent for a while. The waiter served the drinks and left glancing at me for more than the required time.

'So what plans do you have for life?' I asked. A pretty big question for starters. Getting into irrelevant details are such a time waster. I was literally looking for speed dating.

'Work-spend, work-spend. I work very hard for one year and then spend that money on a long holiday next year and then repeat...'

'Interesting,' I said as I took a sip of lemonade. Oh it felt so good.

'And you?'

'I don't know.' I shrugged my shoulders. 'For now, I just want to be happy'.

'Why?Aren't you happy?' He threw a pitiful glance at me so that I start talking and to that expression I broke down.

'Hey, what happened? Are you alright?' He produced a handkerchief from his pocket while I just picked one tissue from the table. 'Stop crying. Your make up is running down your face'.

A typical male strategy to make you worry about ruined makeup to stop you from crying.

'Where, where?' I began to fumble through my purse and produced a compact mirror. *What would girls do without a mirror!*

'Heartbroken or what?' Abhishek asked casually. Bang on he was!

*How do you know? Is it written all over my face or do we share a psychic bond or something.*

'There was this guy…' I started and briefed him about my unsuccessful story.

'I wanted to tell him so many things, ask him so many things… but was not able to write much in that email.' I ended there and paused.

He though briefly and said, 'Then call him…'

'What rubbish! Have you gone mad or what?' I tried to dismiss him.

'Do it'.

Though Komal and Malvika made me delete his emails, block him on Facebook and even erased his number from my contact list, it was amazing how I could remember his number. I pressed the keypad with my wobbly and feeble fingers.

He received my call on the fifth ring right before it was about to reach his voicemail.

'Hello?' He spoke from the other end. I heard him speak after three-and-a-half weeks and I hated myself for keeping a mental count.

'Hi,' I said, my voice low.

'Why have you called me?'

'Because I can't stop drinking about you. Ok,' I said somewhere in between the sobs.

'What? You have been drinking?'

'I mean, I can't stop thinking about you,' I corrected quickly.

'I miss you,' he said after fifteen long seconds.

'Then why didn't you call me?' I asked.

'You didn't want me to call you.'

'Let's make this work.'

'Nitya, you are a great girl...but *kundlis*...'

'Oh please. Don't start with that *kundli* crap. At least give a believable excuse.'

He kept silent.

'Nitya...'

'Don't Nitya me.'

'You deserve someone better,' he tried to soothe me.

'Or is it that you already have someone better?' I asked sharply. Abhishek gave me a thumbs up. Was he backing me or making fun of me?

'Remember when you said that you loved me? I believed you,' I said firmness building in my voice, 'What a fool I was!'

'Could you please stop calling me now? It's over. We are over.' Hitesh emphasized the word 'we' and 'over'.

'I am here all drunk. Ready to pass out any moment. My brain has stopped functioning and even in this state all I can think about is you. And you tell me not to call you?'

'What kind of girl goes out drinking at this hour?'

'What do you mean by what kind of girl?' I asked angrily, 'Ok I will tell you one last thing. Whenever you see me you will recognize what you had, regret what you have lost and realize what you are never getting back.' I ended the call.

'Some people are not worth your time. The faster you realize that, the better off you will be,' Abhishek said handing out some water to me.

I was feeling so much better. I thanked Abhishek for making me call him. He was kind enough to drop me home. Humanity is not lost.

'POOJA AND AJAY are coming to my place tonight to rectify some errors in the big audit. You can come along if you wish,' Rudra suggested.

'But I am done with my files,' I said, obviously trying to shirk off from the additional responsibilities I would get from giving a helping hand to Pooja and Ajay.

'I know this is like extra work, but that will help you if you want to give a client presentation in our next meeting and we could hang out together,' he said. I stayed silent. 'I mean all four of us,' he added quickly before I had any second thoughts.

*Hang out? Did he just use the term hang out? Employees don't hang out with bosses. Bad idea.*

'Errm okay...see you in the evening,' I said, intrigued by how would a boss behave at boss's home? I mean is he the usual Hitler type or would he have a little toned-down personality?

'TOP FLOOR,' I said to the liftman as he pressed button number eight slamming the metal door of the lift.

'Which house you want to go to?' He asked me. Maybe he was watchman cum liftman.

'Rudra Desai.'

'He is at home only,' the liftman said. Of course he wanted to save himself a round of going upstairs through the lift. Too much work.

Rudra greeted me at the door with a smile and a toddler in one arm. He wore a plain black v-neck t-shirt with a washed blue jeans. He looked divine in casuals. His biceps flexed through the short sleeves automatically whenever he used his arms to adjust the baby. I saw Pooja mooning over him in the backdrop.

'Good evening sir,' I smiled back at Rudra. 'Good evening chhotu,' I tried to pull his cheek. Chhotu turned his face away.

'Say hello,' Rudra instructed him.

'Daa daa daa…' Chhotu acknowledged me.

'This is my nephew, Aryan, my sister's son,' Rudra said as he led me to his living room.

His house was not the most stylish as I had expected but there was a certain peace to it. The furniture was minimal and there were floor to ceiling windows which flashed a breathtaking view of the city.

The toddler handed over his toy phone to Rudra.

'You want me to talk to you over phone?' Rudra asked Aryan. Aryan in turn kept slapping his face.

There was no one else at home. Maybe he was assigned the task of babysitting Aryan.

'Ok, *kaun* Aryan?' Rudra asked him over his toy phone. Aryan held his upside down.

'Daa… daa… daa…,' he replied.

'Have you completed the audit of Lalbhai?' He asked Aryan. Pooja, Ajay and I burst into laughter.

We heard more daa... daa... daa... from Aryan.

There is nothing sexier, nothing manlier, than a big guy play with a baby.

'So you guys ready for validating some huge numbers?' He asked the three of us with Aryan still in his arms.

'Daa...daa... daa...' all three of us said in chorus.

'Very funny guys, very funny,' he said.

After going through the tedious details, I was really not able to think of anything else other than numbers. He was right when he said that work will keep you focussed.

After an hour, suddenly Aryan began to cry like a blender without a lid. Rudra picked him up and threw him in the air to hold him back carefully. No sooner, the child began to giggle. Children are such good *dramebaaz.*

I was watching a hulk making tini-tiny baby laugh. He was going to be an amazing father some day.

We laughed and played with his nephew and called it a night.

# Shaadi Mela

'*Aao, aao*,' Malvika's dad greeted us at the entrance of their flat. 'Welcome, welcome'.

'*Kem chho* uncle?' I returned his greeting politely. 'Where is Malvika?'

Komal managed to gift-pack one big box. Her new family had nine members. We got her a roti-maker.

'She is getting ready in her room, waiting for you girls only.'

Komal and I made our way through some aunties clad in gaudy-coloured saris discussing their middle-age health problems and some uncles in plain light coloured shirts discussing politics.

We opened the door to Malvikas's room where the parlour-wali was applying a bright orange coloured lipstick on her pout.

'Hey…' Malvika waved her hand.

'Don't speak,' the parlour-wali told her. She wiped the excess lipstick from the corner of her mouth with her long nail.

'Hey girl! Congratulations!' Komal touched Malvika's cheek with her own as she air-kissed her.

'Thanks ya,' Malvika beamed brighter than the lip gloss she was wearing.

'Malvika… You and arranged marriage? I am not surprised,' I said hugging her.

'Finally yaar. You seem so calm and relieved now,' Komal observed.

'I know...right? Good guys are limited edition these days. Tension tension.' She let out a slow whistle between her pursed lips.

*Why do these girls have to give me a brutal reminder of my single status?*

'Sooo? You got everything you wished for?' Komal elbowed her. 'You know what I mean?' She winked at her.

Apparently during our school days, there were rumours doing the round that a man's private part is directly proportional to his height and since then Malvika had wanted to marry a tall guy.

'You don't get everything. That would be asking for too much,' Malvika said. Clearly not understanding Komal's naughty hint. Komal and I laughed at our private little joke.

'Make a set out of those bangles *na*,' Malvika said pointing to her bangle box.

'So you arranged your love, huh?' I asked genuinely interested, alternating one orange and one purple bangle and slipping a shiny silver one between the two.

'If we plan our education, our career and our finances, then why do we leave love to fate? Tell me,' Malvika said smiling at the guests simultaneously at some distance. 'My decisions are based on logic. As simple as that.' She had a point. Parlour-wali tilted her head upwards to apply some mascara.

'*Achha*? And what if love didn't happen at all?' I asked jingling the bangles in my hand.

'What rubbish! There is no such thing as love-dove. There are only calculations. And I am not ashamed to say that mine is one calculative move,' Malvika said.

'Congratulations Malvika. Welcome to the club,' one of her cousins interrupted us.

'Thank you, thank you,' she returned a genuine smile.

'Ahh my jaws are hurting from all these smiles,' she closed and opened her jaws and repeated this exercise. She saw herself in the mirror and horror crossed her face.

'No, no. Remove all this. This is too much. I am looking like a Hello Kitty.'

'Natural features don't change. I am a beautician not a magician,' the parlour girl gave a curt reply. The two women exchanged cold glances.

'I will see what I can do,' she replied wisely as she knew that her payment would be at peril otherwise.

'Your jaws must be hurting from all the kissing also? Tell no?' I continued on with our topic. There is nothing more exciting to know the excitement of the first kiss.

She blushed.

'Did you kiss him?' Komal asked her in a hushed voice.

'Of course,' she said as she struggled to slip the bangles in her left hand.

'*Waah* only two meetings and you kissed him already?' Komal poked her belly.

'French kiss?' I asked.

'French kiss? Duh. That is such an outdated word,' Komal said.

'Tongue,' Malvika shared some intimate details.

'Eww ... that's gross,' I shook my head in disgust.

'I know, but he likes it intense.'

'What else do you plan to do?' Komal gave her a sly grin.

'No much. Today I will get only learning license. Full license after wedding,' Malvika winked.

'OUR SON-IN-LAW IS a pure gold Hema ben, twenty-four carat,' Malvika's father flashed his son-in-law, 'engineer and ten lakh package. What's wrong? Tell me. He went to Muscat once for six months on a project. We have found a foreign return for our Malvika'.

Funny how Indian parents will categorize their offspring as a foreign return even if they set their foot outside India even for one day and even if it is to neighbouring countries like Burma or Nepal. Now this foreign-returned Kohinoor diamond has raised the bar for my future husband already. So for my mom, my future candidate should have at least travelled to a farther place than him.

'Good good, must say, very well-cultured boy. He even touched my feet. Definitely it must be your choice, haina?' My mom tricked him to know the exact source of this rare commodity golden boy.

In the meantime, the gem of the gems sat on the sofa in the middle of their living room, nodding and acknowledging the new guests of the girl's side.

'Only a true jeweller can tell the worth of a true diamond,' uncle said proudly like he had discovered Jupiter's new moon or something, unknowingly playing right in the hands of my shrewd mom.

'Nitya beta, tell me now…when are you getting married?'

*Aah here comes my favourite question.*

'As soon as you find a good guy for me,' I gave the most overrated reply.

'Don't hurry and don't worry. Take things forward only when you are hundred percent sure,' he replied. Of course he would say that, now that his daughter's line is clear. Not to mention how much hurried and worried he was when he started finding a suitor for Malvika.

'Listen to what he says,' my mom elbowed me like I was an errant five-year-old. 'You were telling where you found him.' She steered the topic back on track.

'Hema ben, we found him from Shaadi Mela,' he said fiddling with his ring.

*Wait. What?*

'Shaadi Mela? Where in Allahabad?' my mom asked innocently.

'Ha ha ha, no Hema ben,' uncle laughed dramatically. 'This is not Kumbh mela. We are talking about a marriage fair.'

'Where people go for bride and groom shopping?' I said.

'Shopping would not be the correct term. It is more like where people come together to serve our community better. Last year it was held in Pune. This year I think it is going to be in Ahmedabad,' he said. 'Wait. I will show you.'

He produced a magazine from his TV cabinet and gave it a pat to remove the accumulated dust. It contained the world's gujju marriage material. He began to flip pages till he reached one. Malvika's fiancé appeared on that page in black and white, smiling like one would smile for a class photo. Uncle showed this magazine after Malvika's engagement purposely. Now that she has been crossed off from the matrimonial market, I was not her potential competition.

His personal information like age, weight, education, address, current job, etc., were written in a box. Those who paid more money had their columns written in colour and bold prints. Magazine was divided into two parts. First half contained the information of potential grooms and second half on potential brides. On the last page some big brand jeweller had advertised their wedding jewellery collection.

'What's your age now? You are running out of time,' uncle asked me. Strange no, how your Indian relatives do not hesitate to tell you the most hurtful things without even knowing that you are offended. 'Get yourself registered for the next mela. You can do it on internet also.'

'Yes uncle, I sure will,' I said.

'Keep this magazine and contact them, ok?' he said.

I nodded.

'See we are simple and good people. Not very hi-fi. What do we want in life? A boy with good degree and stable job,' said uncle.

Now I knew where Malvika got her calculative manoeuvres from. Would uncle be outraged if he knew that his goody boy was a tongue twister?

'Where were you? Puja is about to start.' Malvika's mom hissed at her husband in a whispered tone, 'We don't have whole day. Come!' Uncle walked behind her like he was hypnotized.

MALVIKA AND TANAY exchanged rings between party poppers and flower petals and applauds and jeering. Malvika's mom shed a few tears of happiness as Tanay's mom assured her that her daughter was in safe hands. 'He likes it intense,' Malvika's words echoed in my mind.

Meanwhile Manav clicked the pictures of the new couple from awkward angles to what he described as a candid photography. Malvika's parents and Tanay's parents clicked a whole-new-family picture in an absolute attention position. While Malvika, Komal and I stood next to each other for the photo session. We looked like herbs, shrubs and trees...and in that order, we gave pout poses, mehendi poses and slipper poses, gave some practised laughter poses and threatened Manav that it should come out looking natural deciding on which pictures would look good on Facebook.

Then the quintessential game of receiving gifts and moneys from friends started. After some formal rejections, the couples began to cash in the relatives' blessings. She made a forecast of collecting at least eighteen thousand rupees.

'Oh no no aunty, I can't accept it. It's too much,' Malvika said to one of her relatives who was thrusting eleven rupees in her fist, as the couple bent down to touch her feet.

'You silly girl. You can't say no to this. This is blessing,' her aunty told. Though she gave a mere eleven rupees, but hey, it came along with invaluable blessing. Gifts like these made me believe that we are in recession and the economy is really in trouble, perhaps making it difficult for Malvika to meet her target.

After the gift-giving ceremony, people concentrated on the food counters. They had arranged for a light brunch, calculating that they will have to make the guests eat a full lunch at the wedding ceremony anyway, one of the many traits of the Dholakia family. Gossip session started when one of their relatives broke the news that a distant cousin of Tanay was divorcing her husband. This made an awesome news amongst the relative-paparazzi. It's not unusual for your guests to speak anything about anyone without understanding the delicacy of the situation. Obviously the relatives from Tanay's side blamed the guy and were easy to start with prior judgments.

'BUT WHY DON'T you want to attend the Shaadi Mela?' my mom asked me for the umpteenth time. She was really ready to experiment with anything which got me closer to getting married.

'Cause mom I will have to stand on stage and introduce myself to hundreds of people for matrimony. That's so uncool.' *And unnerving.*

'Uncool? When you will reach thirty, all your friends will be married. You will be the only one left out, then you will remember my words,' my mother warned. 'Uncool, huh!'

We stayed silent for the next several minutes.

'Do whatever you want with your future. You have stopped listening to me since you have grown up.'

A mom's do-whatever-you-want means don't do what you want to do. Do what she wants you to do.

'Fine.' I was regaining my composure. 'But just one *shaadi mela*. No more.'

'You just attend. Only once is enough. You just wait and watch how I flaunt you,' she gloated.

MY MOM RUBBED her hands in glee as we entered the junior suite of Intercontinental hotel in Ahmedabad. It had been few years since she had stayed in one of the fancy hotel rooms.

'You want to order something in the room or shall we go downstairs to the restaurant?' I said as I stretched myself like a lazy cat on one of the extra soft twin beds with ironed ultra-white sheets.

'Will they charge extra for room service?'

'Just order here if you want and don't worry about extra charges. Your daughter earns enough. I can even tip the waiters now,' I said.

It feels so strange when you think about the journey of one by two soups or asking for some free chutney at the Shetty's or packing the leftovers while eating out, now that your wallet is loaded enough to order three course meals and also unnecessary items like salads, *raitas* and *masala papads*.

I browsed some channels on the television only to find the usual suppressed female leads in the daily soaps. First they get married to the hot male lead only out of family compulsion or in exchange of groom covering his face with a flower head gear. But hey, who checks face before getting married! He is her husband not medicines; there couldn't be any complications. How relatable to real-life situations!

Second, they never make out on their first night. Like ever. Then you give that *bechari bahu* a cunning mother-in-law and a scheming sister-in-law. All her blooming youth passes away in clearing the misunderstanding these vamps create between her and her husband. Still she doesn't give them back. Why? Because she is the *adarsh* daughter-in-law. Sometimes I think – doesn't it get awkward when women of different generations of the same family sit together to watch these dramas.

And there has to be at least one severe case of amnesia, one kidnap, a couple of *mandir* scenes, one of these leads this close to getting married to an antagonist character and right at that very moment show the statues of all the Gods in successive clips and because of the severe prayers and penance performed, the other lead reaches there just in time to stop the wedding. How unpredictable! My heart goes out to the male species; they never have control over the remote during prime time.

On the next channel Richard Gere was making love to Julia Roberts in *Pretty Woman* on Star World. I really hoped my mom would stay in the bathroom and we avoid the mutual embarrassment. Watching proper Hollywood love-making scenes in front of your Indian parents can make one so uneasy. It's not fifties or sixties Bollywood where kissing scenes were shown as two flowers cross pollinating.

Seriously how incompatible our TV viewing habits are with our family.

'HERE EAT THIS,' mom handed me a complimentary sugar sachet from the tray kept in the room the next morning. 'Eat something sweet for good luck. You have prepared everything, no?'

'Mom, this is not my science test,' I said ripping the paper of the tiny sachet and dunking the entire thing in my mouth. Sugar rush instantly made me feel better. Now I know why children are fed jaggery before their exams.

'No but still... you always get nervous on stage. What will you say on stage? You do well.' Mom took my last minute revision.

'My name is Nitya and I am not a terrorist,' I laughed.

My mom kept a straight face on my bad joke.

'See mom, don't worry. I am going to go up on the stage and win the world. This daughter of yours will make you proud,' I said like I was going to receive the Bharat Ratna.

THE CURTAIN STARTED acting freaky and a host with the energy raised to the power of cocaine dose appeared on the stage.

'Welcome, welcome, welcome. Welcome Ahmedabad woohooo,' he shrieked stretching the city's name for at least fifteen seconds.

*Please stop! You are not Shahrukh Khan hosting IIFA awards at Macau.*

'Welcome to the Gujarati Lagan Sammelan,' he spoke through his grin. 'People at the back there, please settle down.' The audience became very attentive like lottery numbers were going to be announced. 'Today we are gathered here...,' he said introducing the purpose of this sammelan, who were the founding members, etc. I found nothing new from what was already stated in the magazine handed out to us. The magazine was similar to the one showed to us by Malvikas's dad, the only difference was that this was the latest addition.

My mom caught a quick nap in between. Apparently the hotel mattress was too soft for her and she is used to sleeping on a hard bed.

Boys introduced themselves in the first half.

'Hi everyone. My name is Gaurav Modi.' A promising guy with a dusky complexion and perfect features spoke, 'I am twenty-three years old and live in Gandhinagar. I am a Chartered Account by profession and currently work with an MNC in Gandhinagar.' He wore a checked red shirt, sleeves rolled till his elbow. 'I am Manglik and believe in horoscope matching. Blogging and watching football are my favourite pastimes.' He is a keeper, I decided in the first minute itself.

As I looked around, some girls leaned forward and started making notes in the magazine. I had some severe competition. They were really smart. Well dressed, well educated and I had some serious insecurities.

'He has two acres of land in Valsad,' the father of one of the girls spoke to another, 'each worth a crore at least'. All ears turned to them when they heard the word 'crore'. Once they had everyone's attention, they began to address other parents and threw in some big builders' name to show off.

Real estate is to girls what porn is to boys. One of the girls even made a note 'two crore party' beside Gaurav's name in the magazine. Every girl was judging on the basic parameters like looks, income, social circle, ability to make her laugh genuinely, etc.

'See the girl in front of you. She is pretty no?' one mother asked his son about me, unaware of the fact that I was totally eavesdropping on their conversation. I pretended to flip pages of the magazine.

'She's fat. With that weight, how can she pick up her own weight?' his son spoke. I stopped the urge to look back at him but the flipping of the pages became more violent. I almost tore one. I had also rejected few fat guys in the past. Now it was coming back to me. Karma is such a bitch.

'So now you want a stick thin girl? She is perfect,' his mom told him.

'But I want someone delicate. She is like a *dhebru*,' he didn't hesitate to compare me with a thick Gujarati pancake.

*That's it.*

'Even I have some standards, you *thepla,*' I looked back and gave him such a look, aggressive enough to silence him.

There I was wishing for guys to fight for me like I was the last piece of pizza, and here I was being called a dhebru by one of them.

A GIRL WITH pin straight hair walked up to the stage. She wore a magenta-coloured silk kurta and straight fit denim. 'Hi my name is Rishika Patel. I like to keep updated with the latest fashion and hence I selected my career in fashioning designing. I have played volleyball at the state level and can speak four different languages. I also love to sing and have also auditioned for Indian Idol…'

Every single girl was consecutively replaced by superior category. I was not even their median. They were from leading metros, bold and confident. In fact, when volleyball was made mandatory in my school, the ball hardly crossed the net while I serviced and then there were state level players. It seemed that everyone was doing better than me.

I was having a panic attack when my turn came. My mom asked me to keep looking at her if I forgot something.

'All the best, best of luck.' She acted like a nervous parent whose fifth standard kid was about to perform a skit.

I went to the stage and began to introduce myself. 'Hello all. My name is Nit.....' and then I heard a screeching noise from the speaker.

Everyone gave a sour expression as if they had gobbled down a lemon. The technician took about thirty seconds to adjust the wires. The damned mike failed me. That gave the audience another thirty seconds to stare at me. I have a stage fright and speaking nothing with so many people gazing at you gets me.

Continuing from where I left I said, 'I am twenty-five years old and a Chartered Accountant from Surat. I work with Axis bank. I love reading fictions, non-fictions, autobiographies, biographies, basically anything. I am looking for a partner who is honest and fun to be with. Thanks.'

I scanned through the audience to see my mom lip-sync something to me like I had forgotten my lines. I didn't get it.

'You forgot to tell your name,' my mom said when I reached back to the table.

*Shit! Shit! Shit! How can I be so stupid?*

GAURAV MODI'S FAMILY was standing near the stage.

*Should I make the first move? Why should I make the first move? Why should I move at all?*

'Jai Shri Krishna,' my mom approached them folding her hands in a formal Namaste.

'Jai Shri Krishna, Jai Shri Krishna,' his folks responded.

'This is my daughter Nitya.' Mom introduced me to them.

'Hello uncle, hello aunty, hi,' I said courteously to uncle, aunty and Gaurav, respectively.

'And this is my daughter Sapna,' even before uncle could reciprocate the greetings, another mother pulled her daughter in front of us from nowhere.

Sapna was as thin as a thread. She stood fidgeting as her mom took control.

'My daughter is in medical, physiotherapist,' she said to Gaurav's parents. My mom glared at her.

'Para-medical,' my mom corrected her. 'My daughter is a Chartered accountant,' she said triumphantly trying to impress the Modi family.

'Good good... my son is an engineer,' Gaurav's father swept his glance equally amongst all of us. He played his goddess of justice role well.

'*Arey waah bhai...* I am saying from first only, in India engineers and doctors are match made in heaven,' Sapna's mother laughed to make it clear that no CA, that is me, had any chance with him.

'No no, that is how the older generations think. Modern generation have CAs and MBAs also,' my mom took a stand, not to mention how much she herself had forced me to study harder, so that I could secure a medical seat.

'We welcome girls from both fields, medicals and CAs, isn't it Sumitra?' uncle asked his wife to take over from there.

'Oh medical. No time to learn cooking, no?' Sumitra aunty asked Sapna. Every Indian mother in-law's natural concern.

'She makes amazing tea. You should come to Rajkot sometime for that, not very far from your Gandhinagar,' Sapna's mother answered for her, conveniently arranging for her daughter's first meeting with Gaurav.

'My daughter makes the roundest rotis. We can discuss this more over a lunch,' my mom offered the lunch. Lunch is greater than tea.

*Roundest rotis*? I remember once flattening the dough into something what you would call an African continent. I opened my mouth to say something but quickly shut up.

'How old is your son?' my mom fired the next question.

'Eighty-seven born or eighty eight?' Sumitra aunty looked at Gaurav in confusion.

My mom forgot my height and his mom forgot his birth year. See, we had similarities.

'Eighty-seven, mom,' Gaurav said.

'My Nitya is eighty-five born.'

Apparently there is a general belief in our Indian society that the boy should be at least two to three years elder than the girl because girls mature faster than guys and hence marrying a guy elder to you will bring balance in the level of thinking. Whoever legend told this was seriously not helping in my case.

'Oh, she is two years older. We don't want that much age difference,' uncle said. Game over.

We left as Sapna's mom looked in our direction victoriously.

*Why don't I get these kind of guys? Why do I have to get fat guys? Or gays?* I felt like a loser.

I saw some other real estate expert uncles too make way towards the hot shot Modis.

'LEAVE IT! THAT guy was not very good for you.' My mommy reminded me of the sour grapes story on the way back. 'And you saw that thin girl? She calls herself a doctor? Who will go to such a doctor? She needs treatment herself.'

'See we got so many addresses and phone numbers,' she said separating the pages with her saliva-ed finger. 'Very good. Will start calling tomorrow only. These good guys get picked up very fast.'

*Yeah, we just experienced that.*

I was relieved that this will keep her busy for the next three weeks.

'Have you met someone else?'

'Just met my credit card limit,' I said making a calculation of all the costs involved for this journey.

'We are a perfect blend of modern and traditional values,' Kushal's mom smiled. She contacted us from the Shaadi Mela magazine. Strange, I don't remember seeing them there.

'We are very advanced people,' she said and then suddenly asked me, 'Beta, you like to wear saris or you wear such clothes only?' Her very advanced mom ran her eyes down my sleeveless blue kurta.

'No, no. She wears saris also, but only occasionally,' my mom replied.

'We don't want a girl who wears clothes with leg showing and back showing. No mini-skirts and short-short clothes allowed in our family,' she said scanning my bare hands. *I wonder stomach showing is allowed.* I eyed her sari.

*Oh I thought you don't want stripper as a daughter-in-law.*

'What can our Nitya beta cook?' His mom shot the next question blowing hot tea in the saucer, splashing the drops around.

'Aunty I can cook Maggi, roast papad and stack up a sandwich,' I said frankly, not so ashamed on my cooking skills.

*Maybe I should have said 'What would you like me to cook?'*

His mom stopped sipping tea midway. Kushal ceased nibbling on jeera khari biscuit. His sister almost dropped the dhokla. The time stood still. They looked at each other with their mouths opened (still full of food) and I stopped grinning when I apprehended that my joke went a little too far. I felt guilty for having spoilt their merry making.

'No no... my Nitya can cook basic thali but will take a little while to make varieties. The thing is that all the while she was studying and after that working. Where do children get time to cook these days?' My mommy did the damage control after seeing their frozen expressions.

The patients' breathing returned to normal in our living room. His mom sipped tea which was cold by now. Kushal gulped down his biscuit and his sister Pooja devoured the piece of dhokla which stood still two minutes back in her mouth. Life returned to planet Earth.

'But my Pooja can cook everything. *Undhiyu, khichu, bhadku...* you name it,' his mother flaunted and taunted. At that moment I realised that it was not the silicone implants, in fact it was her pride for her daughter which made her chest swell. I faked an appreciative smile.

'Mom and Gobi 65 also... tell that also *na*,' his sister encouraged his mother to not stop there. *Oh our little Master Chef deserves a tight pat on her cheeks, it seems.*

'Yes, yes my Pooja has joined a very expensive cooking class recently. They teach how to cook Pizza, Manchuria, mix fruit juice... and all. So many fancy dishes, you have to keep up.'

*Manchuria?* I think they need a party caterer not a daughter-in-law.

'Mocktail mom... not mix fruit juice,' she enlightened her.

This is what happens when the groom has a sister similar to you in age. They start comparing. Who looks better, who cooks better, who has a better degree, better job and to top it all, she has a say in everything. Yes, everything means everything, even in selecting your honeymoon destination.

'See Hema ben, I have always taught my daughter cooking first above everything. I told her straight, if you want to do a PhD, go ahead, but don't go to college without making lunch,' she said as if degrees grew on trees and cooking skill was a rare commodity.

Like planet Neptune orbited around Sun, their life revolved around food.

'Aunty, more *dhoklas*?' I tried to serve her the softest ones to distract her mind and palates mid-way. But all my attempts to lure her into temptation failed.

'Today she is our daughter, tomorrow she will become someone's daughter-in-law, then what will her in-laws say? That we haven't taught our daughter anything. If we don't teach them, who will?' The unstoppable woman kept speaking. My mom nodded in agreement.

*What have I done to you to deserve this? Did I wrong you in some way that I don't know of?*

'My son is staying away from home for seven years now. He misses home-cooked food a lot. His wife can work as many hours as she likes, but she has to cook twice compulsorily,' she said upfront.

The idea of 'I cook and you do the dishes' that I was going to suggest, remained a suggestion only. In my mind that is.

'Don't worry, she knows the basic...I have taught her nice and spicy food. We don't like *fikka* taste,' my mom lied in such a convincing tone that could make even a lie-detector machine fall for it.

Joy swept through Jhunjunwala family as the latest news came in. They celebrated it by downing more dhoklas and kachoris. In the midst of feasting, everyone was so engrossed in food that they forgot my and Kushal's private meeting.

'SIR, DO YOU want some coffee?' I asked Rudra as we bumped in the office kitchen. He never visits the kitchen. He always asks our peon if he wants anything. *How did he even know where kitchen is?*

He shrugged his head in denial. I turned by back to leave, and just then, he called me. 'Nitya?'

'Yes?'

'How are things?'

'Which things, sir?'

'Generally. Everything alright?'

'Yeah.' I think he referred to the Hitesh episode. I wanted to steer him away from the topic. 'Sir, actually I was going to ask you if I can come along with you for the client meet with Kapse Motors?

It seems an interesting project and there is so much to learn. I can make a presentation and...'

He made a quick glance up and down the corridor. 'Would you like to come on the ONGC bridge with me today evening?' He asked with a nervous expression. 'Alone?'

The guy who never talked about anything else other than Lalbhai files was asking me out. This was more confusing than permutations and combinations. I stood shocked, my mouth open like I had witnessed a live shootout or something. Say something, my mind told me.

I kept stirring the coffee in my cup, but not as vigorously.

'Sorry sir, I am busy,' I apologised. 'I have to meet a guy for shaadi in the evening.' I cursed myself for giving away too much personal information.

'Oh,' he managed. 'No worries. If you change your mind, then let me know.'

'Sure,' I replied in a non-committal tone. Inwardly I was gloating that I was getting attention from Rudra Desai, *the* Rudra Desai. *If Pooja comes to know about this, she would be jealous like a burnt toast. And if he knows that I am meeting this guy for matrimonial, then why did he say if I changed my mind, I could go out with him?*

THE JHUNJHUNWALLAS CAME home for dinner and the second meeting, in that order of preference. I was given special instructions to cook it all by myself. They wanted a taster from their future bahu. His mom called twice already to finalise the menu.

My mom hit me with a spatula for every roti I rolled.

'Rounder... rounder... what is this? Had I been strict with you years back like Kushal's mom, then I would not have seen this day,' she cursed herself.

'Do you think men want girls who type on a computer all day? They want someone who can make round chapatis. Hey Krishna Bhagwan, please impart some sense into my daughter,' she looked up to the heavens for help. About two dozen rotis were made as a backup, courtesy mom and our neighbour Shaila aunty.

'Girls should learn cooking beta...at least the basics. Look now, what will happen today?' Shaila aunty, our nosy and noisy neighbour rubbed salt into my wounds.

'That is what I tell her... but no. Mom is crazy. Mom speaks to walls,' my mom did not hesitate to insult her own progeny in front of an outsider. I rolled my eyes.

'Leave it. You take two hours to make one roti. Now heat some oil for tadka,' she added snatching the rolling pin from my hand.

I put some oil in a pan to heat and stealthily checked on my mobile for any updates from Rudra. I added some jeera to the oil and smoke went up to the ceilings.

'Oh shit! Oh shit!' I screamed.

All three women rushed to my aid.

Savita ben switched off the gas quickly and opened the windows. Mom rushed to open the doors and as for Shaila aunty, she simply kept advising me in the background. Even at this goddamn terrible moment.

Apparently I had overheated the oil.

'Who are you calling now?'

'Fire brigade,' I said frantically searching for yellow pages and everyone burst into laughter like I was a fool.

'BON APPETITE EVERYONE,' I said with a big grin as I laid the food on the floor. They looked confused. I stopped beaming.

'Is this Bun Apple a new recipe?' his father asked. I stopped the urge to place a palm on my forehead with great difficulty.

'No uncle. It means enjoy your meal in French,' I explained to the food savvy Jhunjunwallas. Their faces remained expressionless.

'Haan...and what has our Nitya beta made?' His mother egged me on. *I hate this dialogue. Each time she says this I feel like feeding her a poisoned bun apple.*

'These aunty...' I said pointing to funny looking rotis and sliced salad garnished in concentric circles. Her face turned pale. That will be reason good enough for them to reject me.

'But what do I do? My food always tastes best when it's cooked by someone else,' I added.

'She is joking. She made everything. I helped her a little,' my mom made a nice backup story. They all gave me a suspicious look.

'Now you also join a good cooking class like my Pooja...you will have to cook *sheera* when you become our daughter-in-law,' my to-be monster-in-law laughed like a bully.

'Aunty, I recently qualified for a bonus...,' I said

'Here here, have some *patra,*' my mom interrupted as she thrust some in Kushal's mom's plate.

'Nai nai aunty, please. I will not be able to eat,' Kushal said almost ready to run away with his plate as mom approached him.

'Why are you eating like a sparrow?' My mom asked concerned about the weak appetite of her future son-in-law.

'Bhai is just feeling shy here. Otherwise green peas kachori is his all time favourite,' his sister butted in. And yes, she was not shy like her brother. She gobbled down everything that crossed her way.

'Why are you feeling shy? Consider this as your home only,' my mom said to propel some more embarrassment.

'Uncle, will you have some more rotis?' I turned towards his father who felt a little left out with my mom concentrating only on the two main people, Kushal and his mother, who ran the show.

'Don't ask just keep it in his plate,' my mom snatched the rotis from me and forced it in uncle's plate. That instantly made him feel significant.

Their family was fed so well that at last even his mother waved her hand along with her head vigorously in denial to any food offered. This means that enough of basic courtesy, they were full.

THE JHUNJUNWALLAS SEEMED very pleased with our demonstration of guest service. Kushal let out big burps and his mother let out even bigger farts. Instinctively, I offered them Hajmola.

They seemed to enter a stage of food coma after lunch.

'Lie down uncle, lie down,' I offered him a cushion and made some space on the sofa.

'Hema ben, we liked your daughter very much,' Uncle said after he got a shy affirmative nod from Kushal. My mom broke into happiness. She looked at me. I turned pale. *I don't want Kushal. I want someone like Rudra. He is perfection.*

'No hurry, no hurry. Let's arrange for a third meeting at our home. Chicken tikka masala? What do you say?'

Me and mom exchanged horrified glances.

'But we are pure vegetarian. We don't eat eggs also,' my mom said. Uncle was suddenly jolted from a deep sleep.

'But we eat everything. We have pot luck party every Sunday and ladies cook fish to have with whiskey,' Kushal's mother said. Suddenly I had excitement rush all over me. My mom would never agree to this.

My mom went inside the kitchen. I followed suit.

Savita ben had already kept four plates ready for their afternoon snacks. Three kachoris, two kajukatris, some chivra and chutney in each. Mom removed one kachori and one kajukatri from each plate and coldly placed it back in the plastic Tupperware box. The ice-cream cups went back into the fridge. The cashews and mouth fresheners went back into the kitchen cabinet.

'Uncle, how about I cook veg dishes and Kushal can order-in or eat non-vegetarian food from a restaurant whenever he likes. He can always have it on weekends. His mom cooks for him on weekends anyway,' I offered a solution so that later mom cannot accuse me for not trying.

'We people are very strict about food,' Mrudula aunty announced. 'She has to cook means she has to cook. If she learns from me now, Kushal can eat in future when we are not there. Am I telling anything wrong?' She turned towards my mother. She kept her grump. Then aunty turned towards uncle. Uncle farted.

Pooja agreed with her.

'No, she will not cook non-veg. We don't even go to restaurants that serve both veg and non-veg food because they use the same utensils for making non-veg food.'

'Ok. There is also no space for stubborn people in the Jhunjunwalla family,' uncle announced getting up from the sofa.

'Why? Has your family become houseful from stubborn people already?' My mom demonstrated her wits.

*Yes, the rishta didn't happen because of the food preferences. How cool is that!*

'GOOD EVENING SIR,' I said when he picked up my call in the second ring.

'Good evening, Nitya. Tell me,' he answered with a little hint of happiness or maybe I was just imagining.

'Sir, you asked about ONGC...' my voice trailed off. I can't bring myself to say that I wanted to go out with him.

'Where are you?'

'I am at Parle Point circle,' I said quietly.

'Be ready! I will pick you up in half an hour,' he said bossily, sensing my embarrassment. I almost hugged myself in happiness.

WE STOOD ONE lamppost apart, gazing river Tapi at ONGC bridge. Till a few years back it was one of the most popular hangout point for youngsters and always stayed overcrowded, but recently that was replaced by three new shopping malls and various multiplexes in the city.

'So how was your meeting?' He asked me curiously.

'Don't even ask,' I chuckled.

'Did you like the guy?'

'No... God no,' I said imaging Kuhsal's mother. 'Why do you ask?'

'Generally.'

We stayed silent for the next few minutes in awkwardness. 'You come here often?' I asked casually.

'Sometimes... to get away from the city.'

'Do you mind if I smoke?' he asked.

'Nope,' I shook my head.

*Do whatever you want. I am not your mother.*

He popped a cigarette in his mouth and started to make concentric circles of smoke.

*Hey he was trying to quit!*

'Are you hungry?'

'No,' I replied in a monosyllable, yet again.

'Do you say anything other than no? No to ONGC, no to food, no to that guy,' he smirked.

I smiled.

'Just be yourself,' he said studying my face.

'This whole be yourself thing is a joke in our country,' I said, 'I mean, what when the entire life we are compared with and taught to be like some uncle's child. Be a doctor or an engineer. Get hundred percent marks, etc. Where is the originality left to be yourself?'

'Ok. So what do you want?'

'I want to break rules, actually.'

'Like?'

'I don't know. Watching movies at midnight, scoring zero in a test with no one yelling at me, riding on a bike at full speed, being a little adventurous... you get the drift?'

He studied my face and thought for a moment.

'Ok, done then. Next week, we will watch a movie at midnight.'

'No no.' I shook my head in horror.

'Yes,' he said firmly. I felt an adrenaline rush.

'I need to ask my... I mean okay, but just this once. 'I looked at him in the eyes and said, 'You seem a lot different like this than in office.'

'Really?' He frowned.

'I mean you are more relaxed like this. Have never seen you like this before,' I said.

'I am like this most of the time. If you spend time with me, maybe you will know more...'

*Oh my god.* My mind refused to look at him.

'Do you go out with your employees often?' I asked him boldly.

He smiled. 'No this is a first'. For some reason his answer seemed honest. *Those baby eyes.*

'Your girlfriend might not like it,' I said. I had given away too much information. Now it was his turn.

'I wouldn't have been here if I had a girlfriend,' he looked at me his bright eyes shining. 'I had an ex though.'

'What happened to her?'

'She left me for some rich prick. And that is when I decided that I will make my life as big as I can and as quickly as I can. You know ex's hate that.'

*No not all ex's are alike. Hitesh would not hate it. I said to myself, without any confidence though.*

'So all your life whatever success you achieve, are you going to owe it to her?' I asked.

'I stopped thinking about her long back. She showed me the exact opposite of what I wanted from a relationship,' he said.

After a few moments of silence, he smiled. 'Anyway... talking about her puts me into a bad mood, let's talk something else.' He then said signalling to a vendor, '*Chana chor garam*?' He asked me.

'Yup,' I said. '*Bhaiya chutney zyada daalo.*' I said to the vendor. 'So what do you do on weekends?'

'Go to the gym, play sports.'

'Sports like PS3?' I tried to mock him.

'Sports like cricket. We have formed two groups in the Surat club. We play tournaments three seasons in a year.'

'Sounds like fun.'

'It is. You should come there some time. Last week only I made my first fifty,' his eyes tinkled when he was talking about sports. Seemed like he really enjoyed it. I mentally made a note to self to wish him luck next time he played.

# Breaking Rules

**Gujarati Parents invite alliance for their CA, fair, slim and beautiful daughter, 25yrs/5'1" Raised with strong cultural family values. Email biodata/Recent photo: ntrivedi25@gmail.com. Call on 98765xxxxx**

My mom posted my matrimonial ad in an English daily. Monali bhabhi suggested that an English newspaper will draw more intellectual prospects. I guess only reading an English newspaper makes you brainy, because no one bothers about your other achievements.

'Hi, this is Jaimin Parekh. I have seen your ad in today's newspaper. I have emailed u my biodata. Can u revert with urs? or u can call me on 98888 88888. Thanks.' I received a message on my mobile at 8.30 pm on a Thursday.

I browsed his biodata. He was an assistant manager in Standard Chartered bank in Pune. He was five feet six inches, had bright eyes and stunning curly hair.

One hour later, we were giving our mini-introduction to each other on phone. He was coming to Surat the coming weekend for training and proposed we meet somewhere.

We met at Shiv Sagar, a restaurant with expensive ambience and expensive menu. He looked so different than the picture he had sent me. In reality, he was at least fifteen kilos heavier. His bald patches at the crown did not go unnoticed either.

'What will you have in starters?'

'Hmm... I have tried paneer tikka here. It's really out of this world.'

He twitched his nose in distaste. 'What about Manchurian? Shall we order Manchurian?' he looked at me expectantly.

'Yeah, Manchurian is fine. I like that too'

'One Manchurian with gravy,' he placed his order, 'What *sabzi* will you have?'

'Paneer bhurji or Kadai paneer. Equal preference,' I replied.

'Nice selection. But have you tried Paneer pasanda? It's damn delicious. We can share,' he asked.

*Have you tried Rogaine?*

'Sure.' *I will make him pay this bill, I swear.*

'Any side dish?'

'Why do you ask? Just order,' I said sarcastically with a tight-lipped smile.

He started laughing and slapping his hand on the table simultaneously. 'No, go ahead. You order.'

'Tadka daal please,' I got to select at least one.

After the waiter left, he asked me, 'Do you have any boyfriend or had any in the past?'

'No, not a boyfriend. But I had a few crushes throughout my education ranging from teachers to classmates to neighbours. Nothing serious. What about you?' I sipped some water. It was too early to touch a sensitive subject like this.

'Actually I had a girlfriend. Amrita. We studied in college together.'

'Hmm... college romances are the best ones. What kind of movies do you like?' I tried to change the subject. Not that I am not a patient listener, but I think it would be more appropriate to discuss private matters after say, the second or third meeting.

'She was really beautiful. But her parents got her married somewhere else,' he kept talking. Maybe he didn't hear me. I nodded my head to share his grief.

'Do you watch movies?' I asked again.

'Yeah, we used to watch a lot movies, that too bunking classes. She has a baby girl now. Very cute, just like her. We are still in touch. She loves me even today and wants to come back to me,' he said with a lump in his throat. This man was seriously lost in a world of his own.

'You know, we share the tiniest details of our lives. We text each other when we wake up, when we eat, when we sleep, when I meet a girl. We are the best of friends,' he said looking at his mobile. 'Hey, it's ok with you na if I talk about her?'

Then it struck me. I must have sounded exactly like him when I met that investment banker. *Oh God, how can I be so stupid!* But I was drunk and this person is sane.

'Hey, you aren't drunk by any chance. Are you?' I asked him.

'No, why?' He was aghast.

'Nothing. Continue.'

'See. This is Amrita. Isn't she gorgeous?' He thrust his mobile into my face to show me a very average looking, but a massive boobilicious woman.

'Pamela Anderson!' I exclaimed and stopped my laughter midway when I saw his expression harden.

'Sorry I was just joking,' I tried my best to keep a straight face.

'Yes. This all is a joke for you na? You will not understand the pain because you have never loved someone. Even she is in pain today. Period pain,' he said.

'STOP.' I nearly screamed. People around us began to notice. 'No discussion about her or her periods. Period.' I said in a suppressed tone.

'And just to remind you, we are here to discuss our match,' I said.

'Sorry. But you asked... that's why.'

'I asked you more out of courtesy than curiosity,' I said.

We spent the rest of the evening without a speaking a single word. I had lost my appetite.

'Why didn't you eat anything?'

'I am not hungry.'

'No. But you have ordered, so you have to finish.'

'I can't have even a microscopic morsel.'

'I hate wasting food. No problem. We can sit for some more time so you get time to digest, and then you can clear your plate. You know how many people go hungry. We are very fortunate, so we should not disrespect food,' he preached. *And how exactly is two spoons of residual daal going to help hungry kids?*

I didn't touch the food for ten minutes. He looked at his watch.

What was he doing? Is he really going to shove the last two spoons of daal down my throat?

'Madam, are you finished?' The waiter eager to wrap up asked pointing at the empty plates and the daal bowl.

'Yes we are. Could you please parcel this leftover daal for this gentleman here?' I said gesturing at the nearly empty bowl.

'Ten rupees extra charge for the packing,' the waiter said.

'Not a problem,' I replied. Even the waiter felt like laughing.

Jaimin produced the wallet to pay; I didn't ask to spilt the bill.

HE MADE ME park my car at a safe parking at eleven at night and from there he picked me up on his bike. I had told my mom I would be staying overnight at Komal's place.

'You ready?' Rudra asked from under his helmet. He rode a black pulsar. There was a *limbu-mirchi* tied near the engine. He wore a green checked shirt messily tucked and his sleeves rolled to his elbows.

'Yes!' I exclaimed and sat behind him. I scanned around to find any meddling relative or neighbour at patrol.

'You should be wearing this,' he said handing me a ladies helmet.

'Screw that,' I said. 'For the first time in my life I feel free and you want to tie me down? No way.'

'Ok, then hold my waist,' he said looking over his shoulder.

'No.'

'It's for your safety, because I am going to drive at full speed,' he warned me.

Helmet or hold waist? No, I wanted this adventure. I had asked for it.

I held his waist with trembling hands but kept a distance between us so that air could pass. No back to chest here.

He turned the keys in his engine and raced, careless about the noise ordinance.

'Here we go...' he said and sped. It was a scene straight out of *Dhoom 3*.

After we were away from the central city, he accelerated. My excitement gained momentum too.

I felt the wind in my hair. I clutched tighter at his waist. I could feel his steel cut abs against my shivering hands. Water trickled down my eyes from the wind velocity. I was smiling behind him all the while.

I never felt more young, more adventurous, more daring. *I should do this often.*

Even when I drove my car at fifty, my mom used to scold me.

'Slow down, slow down. Ok kill me. If death comes, I want to go in my sleep only, but I don't want to sit like this with a broken leg,' she usually said.

'Hello?' Rudra woke me up from my thoughts.

'Having fun?' He asked.

'I love it so much I can't describe'

'Then wait, you will love this even more,' he nearly shouted and tilted his bike at a dangerous level. My left knee was just inches away from the road. Then same on other side. My heart was racing. I screamed in frenzy.

'Want to experience something *toofani?*' he asked. 'Hold on tight. Extremely tight like your whole life depends on it.'

'Oh my god... I am going to die...' I said as I tightened my grip.

'Ready, get set, go.' He slowed down his bike and in one jerk, he lifted the front wheel in the air and drove a hundred blocks like a stuntman.

'Aahhh mummy...' I squealed. He brought the wheel down.

'This is so crazy...' I said in between the breaths.

'One more time, eh?' He asked.

'Yeah. Let's do this.'

He raised his bike once more and drove for another hundred blocks on a single tire.

We slowed at the ONGC bridge and came to a halt right in the middle. The bridge was deserted.

I jumped down from his bike. My thighs were screaming in pain. I literally duck-walked.

'So...how was it?'

'Mind blowing. Why didn't I do this all my life?' I said holding on to the rail and throwing my head back. 'This feels so good.'

'Must say...you are one gutsy girl,' he examined my face.

'And you are one crazy man,' I said. 'I can't thank you enough for this.' I tapped his hand.

'Believe me, the pleasure was all mine,' he tilted his head to one side and smiled.

'Huh?!' I gulped down. I put my gaze down.

'So what next?' he changed the topic.

'Is there a next?'

'Definitely.'

'Will you come with me for a movie?'

'Movie?' I assessed the word. 'Hmm. Movie?' I looked up towards the sky for permission. Sky was my mummy.

'I know the answer actually. You favourite word 'no'. Right?'

'No. You are wrong. Movie it is then.'

'You surprise me,' he looked at me unbelievingly.

This was undoubtedly the most thrilling experience of my life. *When people say that you should live your life the most, they must have meant for experiences like this. Today I felt alive. I want to live like this for the rest of my life. I don't want to meet boys or go to random shaadi melas or be under society's scrutiny. I don't want to go home to a man who may or may not even attempt to make a conversation with me. That is my biggest fear.*

Rudra snapped his finger in front of me. He twitched his brows. I shook my head.

'You know how many stars are there in the milky way?' I asked.

'Millions. I don't know.'

'Even I don't know.'

'That is planet Venus,' he said pointing to a bright shining star.

I laughed, 'Venus is an evening star. You can't see it now. That is North star.'

'There are more than seven billion of us on earth and all we need in life is that one shining star. Perfect for us, isn't it?' He asked. What is it about late nights and cool breeze? Makes one ask deep questions.

'Yeah, but to find that one perfect star, we have to meet so many stars. Or how else would we know that it is the perfect star for us?'

'Sometimes the right star is right in front of us, but we don't recognize it.'

I understood where this astronomy was going. I dusted my hands.

'Office tomorrow. I tapped my watch. My boss is very *khadoos* actually. He will make me work extra hours to complete an eight hour shift,' I said teasing him.

'It's a boss's duty to keep employees in place,' he said softly. Or seductively. I don't know which.

I sat behind him and this time he drove extra slowly towards my parked car. We didn't speak much on the way, but even the silence between us felt good.

'DR AAKASH JARIWALA & Dr Sanaya Modi's Wedding Reception' was displayed on a thirty-two inch flat-screen, as we made our way into the ball room of The Grand Bhagawati five-star hotel. From a distance the stage glistened with alternate strings of fairy lights and small mirrors. White and blue flowers perched on the top making the stage look like a Babylonian hanging garden. Dimly lit crystal chandeliers adorned the ceilings. This was the upcoming five-star in Surat.

We took our place on a round table with chairs that had blue coloured fancy bows tied at the back.

Few days back, I had received an invitation card printed in deep maroon. It was not a simple Aakash Jariwala weds Sanaya Modi but it was the more prestigious Dr Aakash Jariwala (Orthopaedic) weds Dr Sanaya Modi (E.N.T, Gold Medalist). Best wishes from CA

Anirudh Jariwala (Aakash's brother) and Er Tanushree Modi (Gold Medalist) (Sanaya's sister). Below that were written names of other family members and well-wishers with their respective degrees and casual mention of any gold medal achievers in their family.

It was like one degree marrying another. Very trendy. Families of both the parties loved to collect degrees. I wondered why they didn't think of getting married in a library.

'Check this out,' Manav picked up a name plate with his name written on it in cursive and looked at it in admiration.

'Yeah, they should have written B.Com Manav Shah (Accounts),' Komal laughed.

'Where is Malvika? Why didn't she come?' I inquired.

'We are twins. Not conjoined twins,' Manav said.

'Can't you give a straight answer?'

'Tushar is in town, *yaar*. Why else do you think?' he replied as he looked around other tables identifying and air high-fiving our classmates.

A waitress dressed in a black sari uniform handed us an individual customised menu for the evening and took note of our choices.

'Madam, Broccoli soup or Fresh Spinach with mint?' she asked.

*Huh?*

'Brocolli? Is this a five-star menu or a hospital menu?' Manav lost interest in food. 'So much for attending a doctor's wedding.'

'Get me a one by two of each,' Komal said.

She left after taking note of the starters.

'He is a doctor, no? Which specialist?' I overheard one aunty ask another at the adjacent table.

'Bones-doctor, I think,' another aunty informed.

You will be surprised by the efforts a person has put to become a doctor. When you graduate, they are still studying. When you post-graduate they are still studying for specialization. When you get married, they would still be doing their internship. When you start having children, they will start having grey hair and that too without having any fun in life. And that is the very same reason why they are a hit with study books-loving Indian parents. Whatever happened to humanity!

'Very hardworking boy. His mother used to sell tiffins from a one bedroom flat for twelve years to fund his medical fees. Poor woman,' she shook her head in pity as she devoured the poor woman's twelve hundred rupees per plate dinner without hesitation.

'But now look at her…' another aunty pointed her eyebrows in Aakash's mother's direction. Aakash's mother went from all-the-time-tired looking *abla nari* to mommy extravaganza.

'Heard he is going to open a private clinic soon afterwards,' she said. I tried to tilt my chair towards them so that I could come in a better hearing range.

'Where?'

'Somewhere in Kailashnagar.'

Kailashnagar is the medical capital of Surat. Any Sadhu taking a dip in Sangam is what a doctor practicing in Kailashnagar is.

'What? Are you invited? No one told me. I did not get any invitation,' the other shook her head in disappointment of missing a chance of having dinner in The Grand Bhagwati once again.

This is the thing. You cannot invite one aunt and not invite another in your next function if you have already invited both of them in your first. They get very sensitive about it and will hold it against you till the time they are in their graves.

'Let's go on stage and wish them. People are busy eating this food for the sick. Not many people up there,' Komal interrupted my eavesdropping.

Aakash and his wife, the newly married couple stood there greeting and posing with guests. He wore a light blue sherwani with embroidery work colour co-ordinating with Sanaya's lehenga. A heavy camera was set up on a tripod in front of the stage and the cameraperson clicked it mechanically, asking people to look into the lens and smile. People gifting them gold jewellery too posed with the couple. Boxes opened.

I climbed on the stage decorated with a cream carpet. I suddenly became conscious of being watched by an audience and straightened up.

'Congratulations, congratulations,' an uncle ahead of me in the queue wished him, taking both of Aakash's hands in his. 'Happy married life, happy married life.'

'Thank you uncle.' Aakash bowed his head a little.

'Beta, tell me some instant remedy for piles,' uncle asked him for a quick consultation without any reluctance. 'Very painful when I go to the toilet in the morning'.

'Uncle you need to see a dermatologist. I am an orthopaedic,' Aakash explained, eager to fend him off.

'So what? Basics are *toh* same, no?'

'Ok you come to my new clinic, I will write a prescription for you,' Aakash said weighing the increasing length of queue behind him. Our eyes met briefly and he smiled at me.

'What clinic? Now you will go for honeymoon. Then when will I get hold of you?' uncle asked.

'Do one thing, here, write down the name of the medicine on this envelope,' uncle told him, removing two notes of hundred rupees from the envelope he meant to gift him.

He handed the envelope to Aakash.

'But I don't have a pen,' Aakash's voice changed from polite to a plea. It was funny.

'I have one,' equipped Uncle, and handed him a pen from his shirt pocket.

'Uncle, move quickly there are others waiting in line,' an impatient Manav spoke out loud. He grinned at me. I saw a scrap of spinach in between his front teeth. I let it be.

'Which Rajdhani Express do you have to catch?' Uncle grumbled.

Aakash quickly scribbled something in handwriting best known to a doctor and succeeded in warding off the patient from the stage. Now I know the reason why every pharmacist, young or old, has glasses stuck to his nose.

I rehearsed a mental dialogue to congratulate him.

We were next. 'Heartfelt congratulations. You have luck ahead,' I shook hands with both the bride and the groom. Komal and Manav followed the protocol. We collectively handed a bouquet to Aakash and stood on his right to pose for a picture.

'Sanaya, she is Nitya, my classmate from secondary school,' he introduced me to his wife.

'Nitya, Sanaya,' he turned towards me.

'Oh you are that Nitya? I have heard so much about you from the common source, of course.' Sanaya beamed at me and then at Aakash. You could see her gums.

'Really? I hope all good things.' I smiled at her, my eyes quickly moved from Sanaya to Aakash.

'Rest assured. All good things.'

'Looking forward to attending your wedding now,' Aakash said generally. His tone was not oh-you-are-so-single.

'You will not have to wait long,' I gave a tight-lipped smile and moved forward making way for other guests.

The main reason I wanted to get married soon was to prove to Pappu uncle. And show Hitesh what I was worth. And to get away with mom's constant nagging and to stop our neighbour Shaila aunty's wagging tongue.

Ah! That's not true. I wanted to marry because I had started loving Rudra.

'Slow down, madam, slow down,' Urmi from the reunion bumped into me in the bathroom. The floors were laid in black marbles which were in contrast with the off-white coloured Jaguar washbasins. Women excuse-me-d each other to get hold of the big square mirror to re-touch their lipstick or hair. Can't push here too much. A five-star asks for some sophistication.

'Oh hi,' I gave a fake smile. 'How are you?' I said washing my hands.

'Nice nice. What about you?' she asked pulling out a comb from her purse. 'Still with Axis?'

Other ladies watched our conversation in mirror reflections.

'Very much,' I replied pumping some hand wash.

'Didn't see you after last year's reunion. Forgot your old friends or what?' she spoke through gritted teeth, clutching the hair pin in between.

Honestly yes. She was never in my close circle of friends anyway. She was in our opponent's group.

'This is also a reunion. CAs have no life, you know,' I moved to an unoccupied hand drier.

'What are you up to?' I asked. I saw her lip-sync something and then blushing but I was not able to hear her because of the loud noise of the machine. I signalled her to wait. My intuition told me that she must have gotten engaged, or at least committed.

'I have met this guy through my uncle. Things are in the final stage,' she said as we moved out of the bathroom making our way towards the ball room.

*Final stage? This is not cancer.*

'Oh congratulations. That's great news.' I hugged her. My heart sunk. Even she bagged a bloke for herself. 'Who is the guy?'

'His name is Mangal,' she blushed some more. 'He is into IT'.

'Ahan, nice Which city?'

'From Pune. I always wanted to stay there. Better than Mumbai *naa*. I can't adjust to its fast life.'

*But it's still slower than your fast love life.*

'What about you? Still single only?' she asked.

What do you mean by 'only'? When one gets engaged, they suddenly fall in the cream category of committed people and try to single out all the single people, conveniently forgetting that they once belonged to the same nomenclature.

'Yup,' I gave a short and crisp reply.

'Awww… I am so sorry honey. You and Manav are the only ones in our batch who are not committed. But don't worry yaar. Mangal has many cousins. We can do your setting with any one of them.' She winked and giggled. I felt like breaking the mirror into a million pieces so she couldn't adjust her hair without one.

'You have conjunctivitis?' I distracted her from the topic.

'No!!?' she examined her eyes in the mirror and I excused myself.

'Come home *naa* sometime. We should bond together you know,' she said.

*Bond together? You were my classmate who never spoke a word to me when we were in school.*

That reminded me that I had to bond with my current boss, quite literally. It was almost 10.30. I glanced up at my watch only to realize that it needs new batteries. *Rudra must be waiting for my phone call.*

'Sure thing,' I said without taking her home address or phone number.

JAIMIN PAREKH, THE one who still loved his ex-girlfriend called me a week later and talked like nothing had happened the last time we had met. Even I had gotten the time to calm down by then. We kept talking and texting some more that week. I made up my mind to say no now.

My phone rang twice in the lunch break. I saw the number. It was Jaimin Parekh.

'Hi Jaimin! Wassup?' I tried to sound chirpy.

'Hey hi. I had some work in Surat's Standard Chartered branch and I have finished my work a little early and now I am standing outside your office.'

'What! You are not in Pune?'

'No, just came to surprise you. Are you available for lunch?'

Now that he was already there, how could I have refused him? *God! What am I wearing today? No, not this yellow dress. I look fat in it. Even my hair was secured up in a bun.*

'Sure. Why are you standing outside? Come on in,' I said politely and went to fetch him at the door. He greeted me with a frown when I had expected a smile.

'Come. This is my office and that is my desk,' I said pointing to a black-coloured desk and a revolving chair with my name written behind it in bold letters. *Yes, my colleagues are chair-stealers.* Even if you work in a high-profile role, you still have to fight for basic office supplies like pens, stapler, printer and chairs.

'Give me ten minutes,' I said and headed for the bathroom to wash my face and do a touch-up on makeup.

I had to hurry up. I didn't want Rudra to see me tagged with Jaimin. Wait up, what difference would it make? *It's not like me and Rudra have a thing. I am not answerable to him.* But still I didn't want him to see me with Jaimin.

WE WERE SITTING at Hotel Decent which had below-average food. Not many of my office-mates preferred this restaurant; in fact, not even broke people preferred this restaurant and that is one of the reasons why I brought him here.

A teenage couple sat on the farthest corner flaunting their raw display of affection. They were doing some very indecent things in Hotel Decent. We pretended that we didn't see them. He kept his eyes downcast in the menu and I looked at some passing vehicles outside the window.

'Paneer bhurji, tadka daal, one butter naan and mango lassi,' he put down his menu card. 'What will you have?'

'Just one naan. We can share the sabzi. I don't want to upset you. Besides, even I hate wasting food,' I smiled.

The waiter poured water in our respective glasses and left.

'You never told me that you wear specs,' he asked, his face expressionless.

'Why? What's there to tell about it?' I counter asked casually looking at him through my glasses.

'Had I not come to your office today, I would have never known about it.' He accused me like I had betrayed him by keeping my AIDS infection a secret.

'I can't wear contact lenses for longer hours. It dries out my eyes. I have minus two in left eye and minus one point five in right.' I kept my voice low.

'Have you considered that number reducing operation for eyes?'

*Have you considered hair transplant for re-growth?*

'You mean lasik eye surgery? No, not yet. There are cases where the patients lose their eyesight permanently. I am not sure if I can take that risk,' I replied, spooning some daal into my plate.

'Since when are you wearing specs?' *Ok now he is interrogating me like Sherlock Holmes for committing a heinous crime.*

'Hmmm... I don't remember exactly. Somewhere from ninth or tenth standard.'

'Because you watched much TV or because you studied hard?' He laughed at a clichéd question only he found funny.

'I am a Chartered Accountant. I have spent four years of my life gruelling into books when others were watching movies in multiplexes. Before that, I stood fifth at state level during my secondary boards. Now take a wild guess why I wear glasses,' I kept a straight face.

'Ok, ok. I was just joking. Take it easy,' he said tearing a piece of butter naan and stuffing it into his mouth.

For the next five minutes, we ate in silence.

'You look very different from your Facebook pictures,' he marked.

'In a good way or bad?' I asked boring my eyes into him. Any more criticism and I would have upturned cold water from my glass over his bald head. That might have a chance of reaching down to his hair follicles and causing some sprouting on the barren land.

'No, I mean you are way prettier in your picture. Are they photo-shopped?' He accused, yet again. *Did I deceive him into wedding me by displaying my polished photos? Don't we all have our best-looking pictures on Facebook?*

That's it. I put my cutlery down. It clinked with the plates.

'Remember the photo you sent me with your biodata?' I charged up.

'Yeah, what about it?' He replied as offhandedly as possible.

'You were thin and had a head full of hair.' There. I said it.

'But in person it's quite the opposite. Why so?' I said rubbing in more.

Colour flew from his face. He turned pale yellow like a jaundice patient.

'Oh that is an old picture of mine. It was taken some two years back. More rice?' He offered.

I signalled a no with my hand. *I am not going to change the topic that quickly, mister.*

'I had written clearly in my email to send your recent pictures. In fact, you have the same picture as your profile picture on Facebook. Why so? Were you hiding anything?' Call me a monster but I was enjoying it.

'You see, I stay so busy that I don't have time to go to the studio and get my pictures clicked. Will you have some ice-cream?' He shifted uneasily in his chair.

'Had I not seen you in person and kept chatting till I was all head over heels in love with you, then I would have never known. Isn't it?' I put it bluntly.

'Arey no baba, nothing like that,' he mellowed. 'And what is in a photo anyway?'

*Arey baba* is a dangerous combination, mostly used to drift away from the main topic.

'Exactly my point.' I let it go.

He didn't ask me any offensive questions thereafter and I didn't reply with any obnoxious answers.

'So what do you think? Do we meet again?' He asked while paying the bill.

'See Jaimin, I don't like double standards, nor do I want a person in my life who thinks that I have cheated him by keeping some facts. The way you talked today was downright impudent. Since two meetings, we have talked nothing but my appearance and your ex-girlfriend. Where is the 'us' factor? I don't know about you, but for me, this is a deal breaker. And thanks for the lunch.'

I turned in the opposite direction to leave.

'I am sorry if I hurt you.' He said, maybe really apologetic.

'Apology accepted,' I gave a half smile and left.

'I THINK WE are the only ones,' I said as I walked into an empty cinema.

'That's because I have booked this only for us.' Rudra walked up the stairs.

'No...' I stood there in disbelief. 'No you did not'

He smiled.

'Oh my god! How come...how much did you spend?'

'Not a penny really. Courtesy Rajmal group. We are handling their accounts. This cinema is theirs. I spoke to their manager and he was happy to arrange a special screening.'

*A very special screening indeed.*

'Nitya. Nitya.' I screamed my name. There was no echo.

Rudra laughed and smacked my head. 'This is not some Himalayan peak. Cinemas are made up of sound absorbing material and that is why the sound from the movies don't bounce back.'

I walked up the stairs. I chose two premier seats right in the middle of the last row.

'*Waise popcorn bhi hai,*' he produced two big packs. He had gone all out.

'Which movie are we...'

'Shhh..you will know.' He placed a finger on his lips.

The lights dimmed. We stretched our legs on the gigantic couch.

There were no advertisements. After a few introductory clips, I saw the first glimpse.

My mouth went wide open. '*DDLJ!* How did you...'

'Which girl doesn't like it? That was easy.'

My mouth was still open when he popped in a few popcorns.

'A legend once told that if you want to win a girl's heart, then do things *with* her rather than doing things *for* her.'

I almost choked on the popcorn. He rubbed my back. I got an undercurrent.

'Here, have some water.' He passed me a bottle of mineral water. 'Actually I was confused between *DDLJ* and *Titanic,* but then I opted for the former. It has a happy ending.'

'I... I don't know what to say.'

'Say thank you.'

'You know na, you are a gone case?' I asked him.

He shrugged.

The movie reflected my life. Simran's father wanted to get her married to a boy of his choice and here she loved someone totally opposite to her, totally wild and adventurous.

'I love Raj,' I said. I was reaching the bottom of the popcorn pack.

'And I hate him. He has set such high and unreasonable standards for us guys.'

'Hmm... I know. He is a limited edition. They don't make guys like him anymore,' I said.

I had gotten into the mood now. 'First half is better than the second half. So much so that for my honeymoon, I will be going to Switzerland only. Though my husband has not been finalised but honeymoon destination is zeroed down.' I said wiping my hands on the adjacent seats. 'Screw honeymoon. I am going backpacking to Europe next year...all alone.'

One-and-a-half hour into the movie, he rested his hand on the top of my seat. Though he didn't touch my shoulders, but now I could not move without brushing his fingers. Such close proximity. I sat fixed and I kept my eyes fixed on the screen. My heart was beating fast. I looked from the corner of my eye. He was looking at me.

'I need to use the washroom,' I stood up suddenly.

He laughed. 'I will come with you. There is no one out there.'

We watched the rest of the movie in silence.

'You are really spoiling me,' I said as he came to drop me at midnight. I made him park his car a few blocks away from my building.

'A good girl deserves to be spoiled,' he smirked.

'What if this becomes a habit?'

'That's the idea,' he said.

I stood there, dumb.

He sped off after making sure that I securely went inside my building.

# Please Send us your Horrorscope

'Your coffee,' I handed him the mug. We had decided to meet early in the office. I had a matrimonial meeting lined up in the evening.

'One of my very distant relatives, Minu aunty saw me doing bike stunts that night,' Rudra said. That had been a week back. He leaned against his desk and I sat on his chair. *Pooja will faint if she sees this scene.*

'Oh no. Then?' I asked worried.

'She went hysterical. Called up my mom in Mumbai and said that I was holding hands with a girl. Emraan Hashmi *ban gaya hai pura.* Emraan Hashmi doesn't even believe in holding hands.' He took a sip. 'Nice coffee.'

'You serious?'

'Now everyone in my community thinks that I am *Ranjit* the rapist and they want to keep their daughters safe from me.'

'Hilarious!' I laughed out loud.

'Very funny,' he rolled his eyes.

'They don't just get off your back, do they?' I said.

'There are two types of aunties. One who makes you do chores whenever they spot you and another will ask you about your career, girlfriend, etc. The second one is more dangerous. But there is a way to dodge them. Never make eye contact. Look in the bushes, gaze randomly at the stars but never look them in the eyes,' he explained.

'Nice idea,' I said. I made a mental note of trying this on Pappu uncle.

'Anyway, what are you doing tomorrow?' he asked.

This was my third rendezvous with him in ten days.

'I have a plan. Come to Dayalji Garden tomorrow, not later than 9 perhaps. I have to get back home early. Mom is policing me. That day she called had Komal and was asking for me. Komal told her that I was sleeping but I know mom wouldn't have believed her,' I said revolving in his chair.

Just then, we heard a movement at the main door.

'Oh shit, oh shit,' we both fumbled. He quickly opened the door and I dashed out towards my desk.

'Good morning,' Ajay said.

'Morning,' I smiled. *Did he see me come out of his cabin?* I placed a tissue over my head.

'Early bird haan?' He asked.

'Yeah, expecting some guests in the evening so want to leave early,' I said making my way towards my desk quickly.

WHEN I CAME from work, Pappu uncle was sitting on the sofa eyeing me calmly, with a salacious contempt on his face. A pandit wearing those half-moon glasses sat next to him, his eyes fixed on me. My mom sat silently on a chair, opposite to them staring at a random spot, wearing a grave expression. Her eyes were all dark and sullen. She must have been crying. Something terrible must have happened.

'What happened? Has someone died or what?' I said, placing my office lunch-box on the kitchen counter and strolling back into the living room.

'Abhishek's father called me,' Pappu uncle said inserting his little finger in his left ear to remove wax. *Someone please acquaint him with cotton buds.*

'Who?'

'That investment banker through Girish uncle's reference.'

*Uh-Oh.*

'Are you falling into bad habits? Did you drink?' Pappu uncle then put that same finger between his teeth now.

*Look who is talking about bad habits.*

'Mom listen to me...' I turned towards my mom. I ignored Pappu uncle. I don't owe an explanation to an outsider.

'Yes or no?' Mom asked me. I saw a vein in her forehead throb.

I hung my head low.

'*Chhee*! Shame on you. We are brahman. Upper caste. Is this what we people do? Is this what I have taught you?' She went hysterical pointing four fingers out of five towards me. 'You cannot be my daughter. Impossible. Tell me what other bad habits you are falling into? Are you eating chicken and mutton too?'

'Mom please...'

'If your father was here today, then you wouldn't have behaved like this. You broke my trust. Enough now.' She touched her forehead with joint hands.

Breaking your Indian parents' trust essentially referred to three things. You are drinking, smoking or sneaking out with guys.

The pandit was watching everything very silently. *Good he is here. I can say my last prayers in front of him.* I could predict today's doom for myself even without his help.

'Calm down mom,' I tried to soothe her.

'What calm down?' She screamed. 'You calm down.'

'Hema, your daughter is going out of line. Get her married with the first guy you see for her now.' Pappu chappu gave his special shaadi tip. There would be a special place in hell for people like him. He would be punished by drowning in the pool of his own ear wax. I cursed him.

'Nitya beta, before doing such things, think about your mom's reputation. Because of your one mistake, people will question her upbringing only.' Pappu uncle played the think-about-your-mom card to make his political party stronger against me. He is like the bad politician who will sympathize with the poor farmers (in this case my mom) and ask for votes.

He was trying hard to make me angry but I didn't react. I couldn't allow this man to control my emotions and worsen this situation.

'Show me one decent girl who drinks all these dirty things. See Komal. See Malvika and Manav. What a great upbringing they have,' mom said. I recalled Rushabh's wedding and flash-backed Komal throwing up and Malvika doing a head stand.

'*Saada-saati,*' Pandit maharaj finally spoke. All eyes turned to him. 'I study your *horrorscope*. You going to (he meant going through) saada-saati phase.'

'*Horrorscope?*' I chuckled. My mom muted me with a strict glance.

'What does that mean?' I suddenly changed my expression to serious.

'A person life divide-divide. One time good seven-and-a-half years. Another time bad seven-and-a-half years. Saada-saati.' There! The English literal spoke.

'Ok. So now this one is bad saada-saati?'

'Hmm...exactly,' he smiled now that his point was made clear. 'Your daughter very intelligent,' he beamed at my mom. My mom growled at him. Not the time Pandit, not the time.

'So how many years are left for this saada-saati to end?' I asked to shift the topic from me to something absolutely ridiculous. Whatever helps!

He raised four fingers.

For the next half-an-hour he explained me, mom and Pappu uncle various astrological charts and the influence of Mars in the various houses.

'So basically I am a Manglik kanya?'

'Yes and one step ahead,' he said like that was not enough to depress me, 'You Manglik kanya with *rakshash gan*.'

'Kundli not matching with anyone…because everyone manglik but you rakshash,' he said producing a fullscape book and a pen from his Roopkala plastic bag, the one you get saris in.

*He just called me a rakshash...a demon!*

'Manglik people get married either too early like when they are twenty-one or-two or very late… when they turn twenty-nine or thirty,' Pappu uncle said.

'Good, then I have time.' I gave a smart answer to ward of Pappu uncle. He looked pretty dumbfounded.

'No no, my point is that you should not wait. All good good boys will be gone,' he turned to my mom in a concerned tone.

*Yeah right, I have seen enough of good good boys he has shown me.*

'Is manglik dosh very harmful?' Mom showed concern. Thank god she spoke. I thought she had disowned me or something.

'Many many side effects.' Pandit convinced her like it was some sort of new deadly virus in the market.

'She cannot marry normal boy,' he twisted his rudraksh mala in between his fingers.

'What? Now she has to marry an abnormal boy?' My mother's tone was filled with horror.

'No no, you marry only manglik boys,' he said. Of course. Mangalik-manglik cancel out each other. How convenient!

*Boy(s)?*

'Or else?'

'Boy die in six months,' he sounded tragic.

'No no no. Her in-laws will blame us only. Any mother will say that manglik daughter-in-law ate her son,' my mom made her point.

*Ate her son! Who am I? A carnivore? A man-eating cannibal?*

'Manglik person very inauspicious for in-laws also. Business close down. Family disputes. Or one of the in-laws die. Whose fault?' He said. So basically if anyone dies after marriage in a non-manglik person's family then manglik person will be made the scapegoat by default.

He kept explaining one after another the agonizing consequences. It was like a spin cycle on a washing machine. I stifled a yawn.

'Show us some effective solution, maharaj,' mom turned to him for a solution-focused therapy like he was some homeopathic doctor who gave small white sugar candies.

'You manglik so you fast mangalvaar and because heavy influence of shani so shanivaar,' he said. 'Manglik people very aggressive. You do shanivaar, you calm.' So now I was to fast on Tuesdays and Saturdays. Brilliant!

'Correct Maharaj. She is the most aggressive member in our family,' Pappu uncle started his favourite time pass of demeaning me.

'Ok and what am I supposed to eat?' I changed the direction of the subject.

'One meal in evening…no salt… no sugar… and fruits all day,' Pappu mama said. This was pure torture.

'Feed grass to cow on We-nusday, roti to the dog on Thuss-day, rice to birds on Monday,' Pandit said fidgeting with his ball-pen. *Can't he sit straight without any props?*

'And weekend off?' I asked him a sneering question.

'No you give if you want,' Maharaj said, not quite catching the sarcasm.

'Now you have to wear emerald stone in gold ring on your last finger to counter-effect Mars. I will do puja on the stone. You buy the ring from me.' He cleared his throat.

He was talking business. Now we were getting somewhere.

'I will do a yagna and you will feel instant relief. Tension-*mukt*.'

'I make a brand new horrorscope for you. Two horrorscope if you like. One manglik and one unmanglik. Clear horrorscope,' he said.

*Unmanglik?*

'Manglik boy you see give manglik horrorscope and unmanglik boy you see give unmanglik horrorscope,' he spoke. Totally corrupt. My mom widened her eyes.

'Do you give any discount?' I bargained. Corrupt people are always up for bargain. Remember that cop at traffic signal who wouldn't tear a ticket if you bribe him?

'Only if you take whole-sale package from me. I give you free software also for kundli matching. You enter birthdate and birthtime…kundli match itself itself only,' he showed a unique selling point.

'How much?' Pappu uncle asked him.

'Total eighteen thousand only.'

I looked at mom. She in turn looked at Pappu uncle.

'I will call you after I discuss with mom.' I stood up to end the meeting.

His face fell. 'No one give you so many things at this price. You come to me after two days, I charge twenty thousand.' He went into compulsion mode.

'Take it. He is best. My guarantee,' Pappu uncle butted in. *God, this is going to cost me a fortune.*

'My job explain you but you don't follow my advice…not my responsibility,' Maharaj said packing his bag, his face still ashen as

I wanted time to think over his free consultation. He had wasted one hour. 'Something bad influence you if you not doing this puja.'

'Ok no problem. I will see about it,' I challenged. Twenty thousand is a huge amount to spend after a superstition. And something through Pappu uncle is a total rip-off.

'Take it,' finally my mom spoke.

'But mom....'

'Already your drinking problems are in front of my eyes, tomorrow you will start smoking and next day you will eat non-veg. This puja will keep you on track.'

I thought for a moment. *If I buy this then maybe she will forgive and forget about the whole drinking episode.*

'You understand how it affect you? I explain again?' Maharaj asked. I was appalled by his tenacity.

I was ready to go to the library and read organic chemistry once again but I didn't have the energy to go through the planets' astrological position again.

'I understood.' I gave the infamous Indian nod.

Apparently all planets in the universe were affecting me.

'Thirteen thousand.' I started my bid.

'Last I do fifteen thousand,' he said making some calculations on his calculator and showing me the digits. 'I don't get anything. It's cut to cut.'

'Do you accept check?' I asked, tired and ready to retire for the day.

TODAY WAS THE first day and I had to feed roti to a street dog. First, I am damn scared of street dogs. When I placed a roti near the dog, he barked at me. I ran in the opposite direction and nearly ran into a speeding car.

Next week, I bought fodder from a lady on the street who also had a cow standing by her side. So basically you buy grass from the lady and feed her own cow. *Ghar ka paisa ghar me*. Shrewd! I stood there and saw the cow control my destiny, having my fate in her hands, sorry mouth.

'GOOD MORNING, SIR.' I gave a big smile to Rudra. He was checking his emails. He looked stunning in a soft yellow shirt paired with slim fit brown trousers. *The boy's got taste.*

'Oh hi Nitya, good morning.' He smiled back. 'Check with Karanjidas for...'

'For external auditing? Done,' I said.

'Good. Follow up on Lalbhai now...Keep me in loop in the emails.'

'Alright. Would you like some coffee? I am going to make mine,' I looked at him expectantly.

'Coffee would be great. I like mine extra strong.'

'Extra strong coming up your way.' I turned to go but stayed back. 'Sir, you remember naa, tonight...'

'Tonight our date?' He asked. 'I am waiting for it.' He gave a sexy lopsided smile.

I blushed as I shut his door. Pooja was standing right in front of me.

I got a jolt. 'You scared me there'. She looked at me doubtfully. I have to be more careful around the workplace.

SO AFTER MATCHING our '*horrorscopes*', Pappu uncle set up the next meeting with this guy, Ankit, a mechanical engineer. To be honest, this meeting was just a formality. He was already rejected even before I meet him. I wanted Rudra.

He was supposed to pick me up for a coffee after I came from work.

I washed my face, slathered some foundation, dabbed some lipstick, curled my lashes and changed – all in under ten minute. I was about to straighten my hair when the doorbell rang.

My mother opened the door to a six feet tall male version of Dolly Bindra. He was tall like Mt Kilimanjro, fair like snow from the Himalayas, too huge and basically too uncle types for me. He wore a red shirt with a custom stitched jeans. One could see his skin through the buttons which barely came together. If he was ever made to jump in a swimming pool, he would make a bigger splash than all the Olympic divers combined.

'Come in, come in,' my mom said half-heartedly.

'Thanks aunty but it's too hot, we will just have some ice-cream outside.' He said in such a blood-chilling tone that made my mom tremble.

'Of course, of course,' she said.

I placed my hand over my mouth to stop letting a scream out.

'You forgot your mobile in the kitchen,' my mom told me.

'No, I have it in my…' I said as I fumbled my hand in my bag.

'No. It's in the kitchen,' my mom widened her eyes at me, 'Come and take it'.

'Yeah, yeah right. It's in the kitchen,' I said. 'I will just get my mobile, ok?' I told him.

'No need to go,' mom said as she opened the fridge and pulled out a water bottle 'Wait, I will make some excuse.'

'I can't refuse now,' I said taking a welcome sip of chilled water.

'Listen, if you feel scared, or if he does anything, take this pepper powder. I saw it on TV,' she handed me a zip-lock bag.

'Mom that's in a spray bottle, this is in a zip-lock. How am I supposed to strew this in his eyes? Ask him to wait till I unlock the zip-lock?' I went frantic.

'Just keep it in your handbag and don't worry. I will keep calling every half-an-hour to check on you,' she said.

'I will be back before that.'

In my heart I had this microscopic hope that he would have left by then. I wished him to be one of those naughty kids who rang your doorbell and ran. When we came out, much to our disappointment, he was still standing at the door. We both nodded to each other in recognition as I prepared myself for the date reluctantly.

'Bye mom,' I said. We reached to his parked Splendour. I was not going to sit behind him and go untouched. No way.

'Why don't we take my car? You will have to come here to drop me anyway. You can take your bike when you go home,' I insisted.

'No need of that. Don't you like this cool and crisp air?' He said spreading his arms around to show me the crisp wind. But all I could see was stray dogs, trees, parked cars and his bike – Splendour.

Before I could make any further excuse, he put his keys into ignition and parked his butt on the bike, occupying nine-tenth of the seat. The tyre of his bike seemed to be in a permanent deflated condition under his weight. I cringed when I had to touch his shoulder for support to sit behind him. I sat in a pillion position and put my handbag in between us as a safeguard.

'So you are a CA huh?' He asked me on the bike, the wind splashing his spit on my face.

'I can't hear you. Can we talk when we reach CCD?' I said wiping my eye with my dupatta.

The route he took passed through Rudra's place. *Shit. I don't want to be seen with this Humpty Dumpty.*

'Could you take another route? Many potholes on the road.' I said as I tied the dupatta over my face.

'Why are you tying dupatta now? There's no sun.'

'Dust allergy,' I replied.

Mentally I made a note that if Rudra asked me who was I with, I would tell him that it was my distant uncle. Looking at the guy, he would believe me; in fact, anyone would.

CCD STAYED JAM-PACKED at peak hours. I spotted one dirty table and stood beside it to claim. I waved at the waiter but he completely ignored me. We kept standing.

Then Ankit did something unthinkable. He picked up a few tissues and started to clear the bits and pieces of leftovers. My jaw dropped open. What was he thinking? Out of embarrassment, I put my left hand on my forehead to cover my face.

But one thing I must admit, he did a spot clean job. If our maid Savita ben ever took a leave, then he would qualify as our substitute.

'Good job. Well done,' I appreciated.

He felt so proud that he offered to clean my chair too.

'Thanks, but it's ok. Please sit,' I said.

'What will you have?' He asked struggling to fit into the chair.

'Hmm…let's see… hot chocolate,' I said.

He looked around for someone to take our order.

'Oh shit, oh shit, oh shit,' he said burying his face in the menu. Three times saying 'Oh shit' really intensifies the degree of a crappy situation.

'What happened?' I tried to look at him.

'See the person behind me with a little girl? He is my boss. I hope he doesn't find me here. I am on a sick leave today,' he said, his face still hidden in the menu.

I turned my head forty centimetres to the left and fifty centimetres to the right, but he was so big that all I could see was him. I gave up.

Unfortunately, my boss would not give me a leave for neck sprain. And anyway, with that stupendous frame if he thought that he was going to go unnoticed, then he was being very optimistic.

'Boss, one hot chocolate and one cold coffee with hot chocolate fudge and vanilla ice cream double scoop and diet coke,' he placed the order for us both.

'Beauty comes in all sizes,' he said indicating XXL portion of the coffee picture on the menu.

*I wonder why only large people said beauty came in all sizes?*

'So why are you on leave today?' I started a conversation.

'I didn't want to go but my friends dragged me to this Ismail Darbar concert.'

*Can you ever be dragged without giving anyone a cardiac arrest?*

The tables in CCD were so closely spaced that it gave me a chance to speculate him closely. Hair on his body did not discriminate between any skin on the entire body. They grew everywhere, including his ears just like Lalu Prasad Yadav. His eyebrows were so dense, they covered half of his forehead like Yakub, the demon. Dirt filled his nails… ewww. I was not expecting him to be immaculate like Rudra but at least he should have some basic hygiene standards. *God, why am I comparing all guys with Rudra?*

'Why did you choose diploma over a full degree?' I asked. *No, I was not going to marry this man in my wildest dream, not even if I were stranded with him on a deserted island, but I felt the need to keep the conversation live.*

'I am not very good at studies. I failed once in tenth standard and twice in twelfth. Degree *sheegree* is too much for me. And haven't you heard about school dropouts Sachin Tendulkar, Mark Zuckerberg, Bill Gates? They have made it bigger than the guys with degrees. Real life experience is outside the campus,' he said.

*Respect man, respect.*

'Ok. So what do you do exactly?' I asked.

'I repair mobiles and cameras.'

'Right.' I said, 'What are your plans for future?'

'I live in present. Future-*vyoochar* I don't care much. I earn it and then I spend it. Who has seen tomorrow?'

'Ankit, I understand your enthusiasm for life but we are going to live in future also,' I said.

'Leave all that. So tell me, why did you select commerce over science?'

'Actually I wanted to be a doctor after twelfth but did not score enough. The cut offs were at eighty-nine percent and I had scored eighty-five point something,' I said feeling guilty about letting down my mom each time someone asked me this question.

'You could have gone to a private college?'

'They have very expensive fees and for the record not all private colleges are good. I don't want a degree only for the Dr-Initial,' I explained.

'Imagine, just imagine if you were a doctor, would you go for MD or MS?'

'I guess. I don't know,' I replied. *Why is he letting his imaginations wander?*

'Which doctor would you be? Heart, bones or eyes?' He meant cardiologist, orthopaedic or ophthalmologist.

'The one for migraine attack,' I smiled very sweetly.

'What?'

'Which colour do you like?' I asked quickly before he opened his mouth again.

'The one I am wearing, but it makes me look fat,' he said.

*I think it's the fat which makes you look fat.*

By the time we finished our drinks, he pestered me with more queries like why I didn't become an engineer or a sports person or a beautician.

'Is the job you are doing really important for you?'

'Why?' I asked more with a challenge in my voice. I can't hear one word against my baby, my career.

'Is it possible for you to leave your job and become a housewife? You can do some part time tuitions for Junior KG kids or you can teach in Hills Nursery,' he said.

There are times when you are so pissed off that you suddenly become calm. This was one of those moments.

'You do realize that I am a CA, right?' I tried to make facts clear just in case he didn't get it the first time around.

'How much do you earn?' I asked him brazenly. I never do this. I never ask salary.

'Nine thousand a month. Why?' he said his shirt matching his tomato-red face which had lost colour by now.

'I earn fifty-five thousand a month. Then don't you think that it will be more logical if you sit at home and be a house-husband while I go and earn?'

'You have a lot of ego, don't you?'

'I just asked a question, like you asked me.'

'A woman's position...'

'Yes? What about a woman's position? Finish the sentence. I dare you,' I glowered with anger.

He was about to finish his sentence when my phone rang. Thank god mom called. Perfect timing or I would have tossed the pepper powder into his eyes.

'Yeah mom, just on my way,' I said standing up and keeping a five hundred rupee note on the table, paying for both of us.

'Madam, your change,' the waiter came after me with a fifty rupee note in his hand.

'Keep the change,' I said and saw Ankit's face. I felt so empowered. I walked out on the main road and hired an auto.

'What's the need? I can drop you. It's dark already. How will you travel alone?' He said more out of the sense of my incapability than concern.

'An independent woman like me doesn't need an obnoxious man like you,' I said in full Bollywood style and signalled to and auto wala to speed off with me, leaving him hanging in a cloud of petrol.

I CAME HOME fuming and dialled Pappu uncle's number straightaway. Mom kept asking me about my rendezvous with Ankit in the background.

'Hello Pappu uncle?' I howled into the phone, my breathing heavy.

'Oh Nitya beta, how are you? How was your meeting?' He cooed.

'Have you even seen this guy, uncle?'

'Yes? Why? You didn't like him?' He still had the nerve to ask me.

'Have you seen me?' I asked. 'Where did you see our compatibility?'

'Arey baba, I know that he is a little healthy but.....'

'But what?' I stopped him midway.

'Please do me a favour. Never send a guy at my doorsteps without consulting me first. Even better, stop looking for a match for me. Your daughter is turning twenty-one next month; forget about me and please start worrying about her. Show this healthy guy to her,' I said and slammed the phone down.

'Beta, you should not talk to your elders like this,' mom told me gently.

'Mom please, don't start now. And this is not for the first time he has done this. He had sent three guys like this for Pinky also. If we don't speak for ourselves, then who will.'

Every family has at least one scum relative or family friend like Pappu uncle who is not your well-wisher. He was the one against my CA who insisted I choose a home science diploma course instead. He was the one who took my case in every social engagement pretending to worry over my angry behaviour.

*I don't care if I am labelled as loud-mouthed. I can take that anytime over 'healthy guys'.*

'Where are you going?' Mom asked me. I was in the same clothes.

'To cool off,' I said. This gave me a perfect excuse to hang out with Rudra.

'SO THIS IS your idea of a date?' He asked as we drove around the city during late hours in a chariot. I imagined a chariot ride with horse but we managed to find one with mules.

'We are not dating. We are just good friends and just good friends hang out.' I denied his accusations.

'Aah…right,' he gave a mocking smile.

'You like it?'

'Yeah it's different from a bike. I think last when I sat in a chariot was when I was seven or eight...that too with my sister. Fun times,' he said looking around. The high chair made us feel like we were on the top of the world.

'These outings are so much fun. I don't want to get used to it,' I said.

'Why not?'

'Misery is good. Misery is secure. There is no fear of your happiness getting stolen.'

'That is why so many people prefer it because happiness takes effort. Efforts like these dates,' he said, 'and if you are not making an effort to make your life happy, then you are extremely lazy.'

I looked at him like I had just been enlightened. *That is so true. Only you are responsible for your own happiness.*

'Anyway, would you like some ice cream?' He asked.

'Butter scotch.'

Our dates were becoming more romantic rather than adventurous. I wanted thrill in my life but here I was getting more than I had bargained for.

# First Kiss

'Hello?' I answered Rudra's phone in a groggy voice at 2 am.

'Hey you,' he said. 'Wassup?'

'Take a wild guess,' I said like it was the stupidest question in the world.

'Fancy a cold coco?' Rudra asked.

'Cold coco? Like now?' I asked rubbing my eyes. I checked my watch again.

'Come near your window,' he said in a hushed voice.

'What?' I jumped over the bed, awake like someone had splashed a bucket of cold water over my face.

Without switching on the lights, I pulled a curtain aside to see him standing near his Range Rover parked outside my building. He waved at me. I waved back.

'Come downstairs,' he said.

'Arey that annoying Shaila aunty naa, who stays on the first floor thinks it's her responsibility to act as security guard of the building. She keeps a tab on youngsters who come late.'

'Come downstairs,' he repeated with an air of authority.

'Don't order me. You are not my boss here, ok? These are not office hours.'

'I will always be your boss...here, there and everywhere, whether you like it or not.'

'Oh yeah...? Wait.' I put on my slippers and tip toed out turning the spare key as silently as possible at the risk of waking up my mom. I pulled apart the metal doors of the building and locked it again.

'Get in, quick,' he said as he pressed the button on his side to open the door for me. I looked around to see if Shaila aunty was peeking through her windows and slipped in the seat next to him.

He was in his tracks and his hair was just out of bed type. He looked super sexy. I felt like running my hand in them.

'Quick, quick, start the car, start the car. Or else someone will catch me red-handed with you,' I said as I sunk in his seat to hide my face. 'Where are we going by the way?'

'A-one coco. Only place open this late.'

'HMM SO THIS is what you wear at night?' he said checking out my Minnie mouse t-shirt and pink shorts to match. 'Don't get out of the car. I will get Kaju Coco for you here.'

'I can't have anything now.' I shrugged my shoulders.

'Why not?'

'Shanivaar.'

'You fast on shanivaars?' He was not able to contain the surprise in his voice.

I nodded.

'That pandit told me... so that I get a good husband.'

'That *toh* you will get even without fasting,' he said.

*Why does he talk in double meaning?*

'Since I am breaking all protocols this week I will have a cold coco. But I want to sit in the restaurant and have. Not like this in the car,' I said making a baby face.

'No. You sit in the car,' he said eyeing some loafers outside.

'Why not?' I asked as innocently as a lamb. I exactly knew why not. But sometimes it's kind of fun to piss him off.

'Because I don't want you to parade in front of those scavengers in these inappropriate clothes,' he howled, pointing towards some guys doing stunts on their bikes.

Ok girls get it that their guys can see what goes in the mind of other guys when they see a scantily-clad girl which sometimes a girl fails to notice and believe it or not but girls like it when guys get protective.

'*Yeh kaali kaali aankhein*,' one of the loafers who looked like the leader of the gang began to circle our car in an imaginary orbit on his bike.

'*Tu ru ru..tu ru ru*,' his fellow gangsters provided the chorus.

'*Kya hai*?' Rudra forbade them. The same tone in which he warns us to give overtime if we don't complete our files within the given deadline.

'Nothing. It's too late so was asking your sister if she needs a ride back home?' Dawood Ibrahim spoke tapping the backseat of his bike while all the Abu Shakeels laughed dutifully on his bad joke. *See it's not just us laughing on our boss's stale jokes. These things are prevalent everywhere, even in an underworld organization.*

'Just get lost ok.' Rudra said curtly signalling me to close the window on my side. He started to take reverse.

'Being a hero to impress the girl, eh? Come outside the car and I will show you who I am.'

Rudra stopped the car midway. I pressed Rudra's hand. My second body contact with him.

'I need to teach him a lesson,' he said at him sharply. 'Don't worry. I can take care of myself. I was involved in a lot of street fights while growing up.'

'Dawood Ibrahim is needling you. He wants you to get out of car and then reach me. This will put both of us in trouble. Let's go.'

He thought for a second.

'You want to go?' His expression suddenly changed from serious to playful, 'Ok let's go.'

He put the keys in ignition and quickly changed the gear from two to four passing extremely close to the main villain, knocking him off along with his two assistants before we sped off. We saw them lip-sync a few cuss words behind us. We burst into laughter while he drove onto the main road.

'Whoa. Never knew this side of you,' I widened my eyes.

'Should have knocked down the other two as well,' he said grinning like a teenager.

I don't know if it was a romantic breezy night or it was the thrill of dodging a goon, but he suddenly placed his hand on mine. A shiver ran down my body. *It's amazing how after midnight if you speak to someone, you become extremely personal and it's weird.*

Rudra Desai, the hottest man I had ever seen, who the girls would kill to be with had his hand on mine.

Maybe it was casual. Maybe he had placed his hand on everyone's. Or maybe he liked my hand. I don't know but at least I liked it.

He used his right hand to change gears also, because he didn't want to let go of my hand. I gently pulled my hand away and acted like nothing had happened. The inside of my heart accelerated to a million beats per second.

'Thanks for the good luck message for the match, by the way. It meant a lot,' he said, his focus on the road.

*Sleep will desert me tonight.*

MY MOM'S *MAMI ki jethani ki bahu* hooked me up with a hot-shot guy at Holiday Inn. Apparently even she was concerned about my wedding. And today was the first time I had heard about her.

*Who are all these people? Why are they keen on setting me up? How are they getting information about me and my single status?*

Vismay Rana was the young leading manufacturer of diamonds in the city. Everybody in Gujarat knew his name. His articles regularly published in Gujarat dailies. Every now and then, local channels interviewed him. He had inherited an import-export business and was seriously good at expanding it. He had done his Master's in Business Management from some unknown university in London. He was fair-skinned, had jet black hair swiped in one direction and came to meet me in a business suit. There he was sitting in front of me all corporate looking, messaging someone on his Vertu.

'I have to meet a client from Israel directly after this meeting. So we better keep this meeting short and simple and come straight to the important questions,' he said glancing at his watch.

*Wow, no one had introduced himself to me like that before. Fair enough. My time was equally important. Let's try this no-time-wasters meeting also.*

'So I am hoping you must have already done some research about me, right?' He asked me.

*Research about you? Why, are you a university paper?*

'No. Not much,' I lied impassively. He gave me an arrogant smirk.

'Ok then. I will introduce myself. You are talking to one of the richest and the most successful diamond tycoons of Gujarat. We deal in import export of diamonds from around the world. I have companies in six countries across Europe and the seventh one is under construction in Dubai as we speak.'

*Yes, please continue while I take note, Mr Brag-may Rana.*

'Our close circuit of friends and family includes some well-known members of the parliament and other influential people,' and my God, he continued.

*Whatever happened to keep-your-feet-on-ground modesty.*

'So?' I just asked a simple question after he narrated me an essay on him.

'So?' He repeated my question in confusion. Maybe this was not the response he was expecting from me. Maybe because I didn't bow down and touch his feet.

'So how does this relate to our compatibility or you being a partner I am looking to spend my life with?'

The richest person on the soil of Gujarat looked a little dumbfounded.

Just then the waiter opened a bottle of Aquafina, poured the water in the glasses and handed us the menu cards. I went through the starters and giggled.

'Something funny?'

'This is how you will read a Bhel Puri if you go for a fine dining,' I laughed, stopped to breathe and then laughed again, 'House favourite! Home-made crushed crispy pastry seasoned with hand-picked potatoes and puffed rice coated in the goodness of sweet and sour tamarind sauce, sprinkled with thinly fried gram flour sticks and garden fresh cilantro and mixed spice.'

He was staring at me, expressionless. 'I mean come on... it's just a damn Bhel Puri and they make it sound like I was eating what would be put on the plate of Queen Victoria,' I said.

'Keep your voice down. This is not your local café. This is a five star,' he said in a hushed voice. 'And besides, if you want to be my wife, then you will have to get used to these things.'

Colour drained from my face.

'Yeah, I know that,' I replied curtly. 'Not my first time in a five star.'

I thought for five seconds and since this was a no-time-wasters meetings, I came straight to the point.

'What kind of partner are you looking for? Do you have an image in your mind?'

'Of course I always have my blue prints ready whether I have to pitch a potential diamond merchant or my marriage partner,' he said. 'See I want someone who can gel very well in my social circle.'

'Ahan,' I was listening.

'My preferred partner will accompany me to our annual meetings and other business parties. She should look good all the time, will just have to give menus to the cooks and order servants for the general maintenance of the house and look after the family and kids.'

*Oh you didn't imagine her to massage your legs after you come home tired from work.*

'What if she is working?'

'Then she will resign.'

'Oh. But mom's mami's jethani's bahu said that you wanted a highly educated girl.'

'Of course. I can't marry just a graduate. What would people say? Think about my status at least.'

'But what about my job then?'

'You women don't worry about jobs and business. You just have fun. Go to malls. Shop. Enjoy life, you know. Leave all those kind of tensions for us.'

'But I enjoy being a CA and you think that I am not capable of handling a business?' I asked him. I started taking long deep breaths, one of the yoga techniques I saw on TV to calm down. I signalled the waiter to fill up the glass with water.

'That all I don't know and I don't care. All women in our family are like that and I am going to maintain that standard.'

'So basically you want a trophy wife?'

'Yeah, if you want to put it that way.'

'I am not going to leave my job after marriage. No way,' I shrugged in a steely resolution.

'Job?' he laughed like it was a berated word.

'How much do you CAs earn? Fifty thousand? Sixty thousand? Seventy thousand a month?' He opened his palm to gesture the amount. 'I deal in crores every single day, just like this,' he snapped his fingers.

'Think of my public image, my reputation. What will people say when Vismay Rana, the brand, has a wife working in some stupid bank.'

Shah Jahan cut the hands of his workers after they built Taj Mahal for him. I felt like chopping off his fingers after he was building the slow anger in me.

'Why don't you stay at home and look after the family and I will transfer one lakh rupees into your bank account each month. Consider that as your salary.'

He had the capacity to make my blood boil even in an air conditioned airy room. I deliberately lifted the fork and knife as a warning when I spoke to him. That moron thought that I was going to have my bhel puri with knife and fork.

Forget about a decade, I think that this person is from a different century altogether.

'Listen, you primitive man,' I pointed my fork towards him. 'Were you looking a lot out of the window during your history class?'

'No. Why?' he looked at me aghast.

'No because this is not the stone age where men are hunters and women are gatherers,' both I and my voice rose. I left sooner than I expected.

He later gave my detailed review to my mom's mami's jethani's bahu which soon spread in my whole clan that I am too modern, too obnoxious and have lost my way. Chartered accountancy has got into my head and that he has ten people like me working for him and that I won't pay respect to elders by doing a full time job. *Huh?* Pappu uncle had a gala time.

I didn't care less. I would rather stay unmarried for seven births than marry that Vismay Rana.

'SEE THIS GUY… your future son-in-law.' I said pointing at the computer screen. Ankit, the guy who I had met at Café Coffee Day had sent me his matrimonial biodata again.

She came hurriedly and her expression turned into distaste when she saw him. I suppressed a chuckle.

I said casually, 'By the way, his father called in the morning. I told him that we don't want to proceed. He asked what was the problem with his son. He has a diploma, a job, is fair and handsome..'

'I replied that your son is a diamond but there will be height issues,' my mom said.

'How do you do this email?' She asked reaching for her glasses, 'Teach me also.'

I SWITCHED ON the lights in the living room and threw the keys on the coffee table. My mom was awake and speaking to someone over phone. She looked disturbed. I turned the speaker on.

'But aunty, what problem do you find with me? Tell me?'

'I told you once and am repeating it again, my daughter is simply not interested in you *bhai*,' she said her voice changing from a plea to frustration.

'She had some misunderstandings about me in our first meeting. I want to clear the air.'

'The air was clear when you met her the first time…'

I gestured and asked her if she wanted me to speak to him. She shook her head in denial.

'Fine. You know what aunty? Now I reject your daughter. I don't want to get married to her,' he vented. 'Go and find someone who could be a better son-in-law than me.' Saying that, he slammed the phone.

*Yeah right!*

I rolled my index finger next to my temple to gesture to mom that he was a crazy guy.

'Such a weirdo!'

'Did you see? How he talked to me?' my mom cried in outrage.

'Good riddance,' I said as I switched on the computer.

'I am not giving my daughter to him. Who is he to refuse you?' My mom na, really cannot handle rejection.

'Good no? Now we don't have to find any silly excuse,' I said as I checked my mail.

*From: Ankit Modi*

*Subject: Declaration of rejection*

*I caled u to clear confusion bt seems u r not interested in dis opotunity.*

*So hereby I declare dat I have rejected u. u will never find n e gud guy lyk me. Bye*

This guy has gone bonkers. I think he is going to reject me in fifty thousand ways. I brushed his thoughts away and decided to login to all three matrimonial sites. I wanted to deactivate my account. I got a notification from bharatmatrimony with a sad smiley that Ankit Modi has declined my interest. *Man, he is real fast.*

'Hello.' I got a call from an unknown number on my mobile the next day when I was just about to leave for work.

'Hello, who is this? Nitya?' I heard a male voice from the other end.

'Yes, *aap kaun*?'

'Hi, this is Ankit.'

'Ankit....' I browsed my memory.

'We talked about matrimony yesterday,' he said.

'Yes, tell me,' I said rolling my eyes.

'Why did you refuse to meet me?'

'Listen, I am getting late for work and I have more important things to do. Can we talk later?'

'Ok take my number,' he said.

'I don't have a pen,' and without even waiting for his response I pressed end call and left.

I was jet-lagged from the late night dates with Rudra. I was neck-deep in files at office. I skipped both my breakfast and lunch and looked like I would have to skip my dinner too if I did not finish it in time. Stupid Ankit kept calling me throughout the day to increase my worries and woes. What did he want now? Did he want to reject me on phone? The watchman came to me and said, 'Madam there is someone outside waiting for you.'

'Who?' I asked without breaking my gaze from the computer screen.

'Would not say his name. Is saying that madam knows me.'

'Tell him to wait, I will be out in a moment,' I said.

Ten minutes later, I went to the reception. Shit, it was Ankit sitting there reading *Femina*. He wore a skin tight fake Puma t-shirt with an even tighter jeans. You could literally see the shape of his crotch. His face was way bigger than the rest of his body like a football on a badly shaped matchstick. I turned my gaze away.

'Hi. Ankit,' he extended his hand.

'What are you doing here?' I asked sternly, keeping my hands folded across my body.

'Do you have a problem with me?' he asked me trying to pin me down with his eyes.

'How did you get my office address?' I kept a steady tone.

'I know where Axis Bank, Nanpura branch is. Everyone knows where Axis Bank is,' he said throwing his arms in air and tilting his head simultaneously. I made a mental note to remove the name of my company from the matrimonial biodata and from everywhere I had uploaded it.

'Why did you reject me? What's wrong with me?' he raised his yakub eyebrow and widened his eyes. 'Oh now I understand. You like to play the chase huh?'

*I am playing leave me the fuck alone.*

'This is not a good time. I am busy. I will speak to you later,' I kept my voice low and turned to leave. We were already getting undue attention from receptionist, watchman and two colleagues.

'No, tell me now. I am not going anywhere without an answer..'

'Because I don't like your personality. Ok?' I cut him in between.

'And I don't like your face. Ok?' he said loudly pointing his finger at me.

I was stunned. Even the rest of the staff gathered in the reception area when they heard him scream. Even the security guard came running with his gun.

'Don't create a scene here,' I spoke through gritted teeth.

'You know what? Now I reject you. Heard it? I. REJECT. YOU. Ankit Modi rejects you,' he said stressing each and every word, wagging his inked finger ferociously at me. 'That too in front of your colleagues, I reject this woman as my life partner.' He banged his fist onto his other palm. By this time, he was out of breath, trembling with anger.

'I heard you the first time,' I said keeping my voice low.

*Well played. He made it look like I was stalking him to inflame his bruised male ego in front of people. What a loser!*

'What the hell is going on?' Rudra stormed out of his cabin, 'Who is this prick?' he turned towards Ankit.

'Hey who are you calling a prick, eh?'

'You,' Rudra said staring right into his eyes. 'If you want to create a scene, go somewhere else. Not here, ok. This is a professional place.' His tone was a warning.

'I need to sort something out with her,' Ankit said pointing his chin towards me.

'Not now. This is her work time,' Rudra said sternly. By this time everyone had gathered around us. 'Please show yourself out.'

'Don't you ever call me.' He stomped his foot on the ground and raged out of the door.

From the corner of my eyes, I could see that my colleagues were giggling and whispering something to each other.

'Nitya, come inside my cabin!' Rudra went back.

'Movie finish. Get back to work,' I said sarcastically. 'By the way, he was just an eve teaser,' I added. I felt the need to give an explanation.

'Who is he?' Rudra asked me, his eyes burning. He looked hotter when angry.

'A guy I rejected for shaadi,' I gave a clipped answer.

'Why are you meeting guys for matrimony?' he asked me, his eyes burning.

'Why shouldn't I meet guys for matrimony?' I bore my eyes right back.

'Is he harassing you?' His expression changed to concern. Inwardly I gloated that he cared about me but then he must be caring for all.

'Err...' my voice trailed off.

'You are not going home alone tonight. I will drop you,' he announced rather than asking.

'Thank you,' I murmured weakly. A little security could help.

That night on the way, Rudra spoke only in monosyllables. He was mad and he had every right to be mad at me. To ease the tension, he stopped near an ice cream vendor and feasted on some really good kulfi.

He stopped his car on an empty street. He took a deep breath, like he was trying to cool down. Then his expression became softer when he looked at me.

'You have the most extraordinary eyes I have ever seen. Are they brown or hazel?' Rudra asked. I think he complimented me only to make an eye contact because I was looking everywhere but at him.

'Actually they are grey just like Sushmita Sen, a rare colour,' I said, quickly changing my glance from him to the roadside beggar who I felt was just pretending to sleep, waiting for us to make out or something. I suspected he had a camera to make an MMS.

Had it been any other situation, I would have squinted at Rudra and laughed, but not today. I couldn't murder this moment. And to bring out romance from a person like me, who is either comic or sarcastic most of the times is a must watch. Had Komal, Malvika or Manav seen the coy version of me, they would have died out of laughter. I was used to mercantile laws and quantitative aptitude, but not this kind of extra-curricular activity.

'I like your lips,' he brushed his fingers against my lips. I turned my face away.

'How many guys have you kissed before?' He asked with a hint of jealousy in his voice.

'I have never been kissed. Wanted to save it for someone special.'

This thing with Rudra felt so different and I hated to admit it, but equally good too.

'Never?' he smirked and I had that uncanny feeling that he was laughing at me. I shook my head.

He came dangerously close. He entered the territory where no guy ever had. He smelled of musk. I chanted the Gayatri Mantra.

When he was just a few decimal points away, I forgot to breath. I held my heart in my mouth. I kept my gaze down, not at him, not out of the window, not at the beggar, but down, down at my hands which were firmly clasped together.

Just when I thought he was going to kiss me on my lips, he tilted his head and kissed my neck under the right ear. His kiss made a sound, a sound as sexy as his voice. My heart raced at hundred and fifty miles per hour. I placed my hand firmly where he had kissed me.

'I want to go home,' I said like a child who was perhaps about to be kidnapped by a stranger.

'What?' He asked perplexed, pulling his head away.

'Just take me home.'

'Ok, ok relax,' he didn't argue but put the keys into ignition. He turned on the radio and started humming the tune. On the whole journey way back home, we remained silent. I just looked outside the window in the direction opposite to him. I could have gotten a a neck sprain, but I kept looking out.

He stopped his car a few yards away from my building. 'I hope you enjoyed it cause I sure did,' he said in a low voice.

'*Achha*? The ice cream or the kiss?' I asked looking right into his hot smouldering eyes this time. Yes, I became more confident as I was right outside my building and I could run towards home any moment.

Once again he came very close to me, and this time too, his lips turned towards my ear.

'Both,' he whispered in the most seductive voice I had ever heard. I turned the brightest shade of crimson.

'Gotta go. Can't pull an all nighter,' I said quickly and kept walking without looking back. I dared not look into those eyes.

'We hardly reach somewhere and you always gotta go.' I heard him speak behind me.

I went back to my window to find him still waiting for me to return to my room before he sped away.

# Shaadi Brouhaha

While on the office front, although me and Rudra kept the safe distance in office, the chemistry between us was electrifying. Completing audit, valuating businesses, and PowerPoint presentations seemed irrelevant despite the peak season.

'Everyone,' Rudra clapped his hands, 'meeting in my cabin in five minutes.'

We all stood in a semi-circle in Rudra's cabin for the morning mass drill, me standing exactly opposite to him. He wore a crisp white shirt with his trademark perfect fit. *Despite the chaos, how does he manage to look so immaculate? Who does the shopping for him?*

'Pooja, have you discussed about the information and deadlines with Bhupendra Advocate about First Event Management company?' He leaned on his desk and started delegating duties.

'Sir, I have spoken to them, they need more time,' Pooja said fidgeting with her pen.

'That's the thing. We don't have time,' Rudra shook his head. 'Or contact Kapadia lawyers and sort it out. You are not going home without getting it done. Ok?'

'Yes sir,' she said meekly, fluttering her mascara-heavy lashes. Rudra on other hand seemed oblivious to her charm.

'Have you processed and analysed the documents for Shalimar restaurant?' He turned to Ajay, simultaneously making notes in his diary.

'Almost done sir, I need only one hour,' Ajay said like he was all ready with a camera for a sting operation. Rudra nodded.

'Nitya,' he quickly scanned my face and then a quick look at my neck where he had kissed and then dug his eyes into his diary, 'Have you finished the Audit for Lalbhai?' I had a feeling that he suppressed a smile.

'Lalbhai case is complete and so is M K Shah, sir.' I stressed at the word 'sir'.

'Well done,' he told me. All three of us looked at him in shock. He had never appreciated any employee in all these months. Had our pervious boss Rakesh sir had said 'well done', it would not have been counted, but coming from Rudra meant so much. *Was it a special favour or was he referring to the kiss or did I really do a good job.* Pooja's face looked like a burnt cigarette ash.

I gave him a tight lipped professional smile.

'Help Ajay for audit of Shalimar after he is done with the analyses and till then, help me with my documentation,' he ordered keeping his eyes buried in his notes.

'Ok so that's it. Get back to work,' he said hurriedly looking at Pooja and Ajay to vacate the room for us.

'What happened?' He shut his book, 'You have been distant since the sexual harassment?' Rudra flirted referring to the kiss, as soon as Pooja and Ajay left.

He looked as handsome as Michelangelo's David. I felt like cloning him.

'You are committing human resource violation, sir.' I answered playfully, 'I can sue you for this.'

'Of course you can, but for that I will have to exploit the rules to the fullest first,' he said as he neared me.

'Stop. One arm distance, one arm distance.' I said raising my hand in front of him and looking around. The blinds were shut. 'I don't know about Ajay, but Pooja is surely not dumb.'

'I want to kiss you,' his voice was husky as he approached me, 'and not on the neck this time'.

I placed my hand on my neck in a reflex.

*You want to kiss? Again?*

'No, no,' I said terrified, 'I can't.. I'. My voice trailed off as I looked down.

'No..no.. no.. it's your favourite word, isn't it?' He said. 'Ok then I won't let you leave this office till late night and then I will have to drop you home and will kiss you anyway,' he backed off.

I felt energy rush to my head. I held the door knob for support.

'I... I... I should be working.' I left feeling nervous and excited at the same time.

'WHAT'S THE SCENE between you and him?' Pooja asked with her eyebrow raised. *She needs to get her eyebrows threaded.* We met near the office printer during lunch hour otherwise it's always occupied.

'What are you talking about?' I asked her.

'Don't act. I know there is something going on between you and Rudra sir,' she said

'Watch what you say before pointing a finger at someone. And for the record, there is nothing going on between me and him and even if there is something, then it's none of your business,' I shoved her off. I don't want to give a breaking news to office paparazzi.

The day was busy and hectic. I bumped into Rudra many times that day. I blushed strawberry pink every time. And after I finished my work, I left silently. I knew he wanted to kiss me and I couldn't let him do that just as easily. Again, Pooja was observing my every move, so today was not the day. He will have to wait till the storm is cleared before he gets me.

I CALLED UP my gang at Z2000 to have a bowling evening and also to inform them about Rudra. After what had happened last time, I had to share it with them this time.

'I want to get committed.' Manav dropped a hand grenade on us. 'After fifteen girls having friend-zoned or brother-zoned me, I want to get committed.'

'What? You want to get committed with someone else? So suddenly I am not good enough for you?' I said tragically tying up my shoe lace.

Manav gave me an air kiss.

'Who's the chic?' Komal asked him testing her strength against various metal balls.

'Yogeshwari.'

'What? You have met that girl like a few hours ago,' Malvika said utterly shocked.

'Say a few days at least. Anyway, yesterday something happened which has changed how I feel about her,' Manav was surely not expecting a lukewarm response.

'Is she going to father your child? Tell me...' Malvika asked him doubtfully.

'No yaar. She doesn't let me do anything more than kissing,' he said picking up a yellow ball.

'The other day I was planning a vacation with her to Kerala and guess what she said? Even in my wildest dream I didn't know that she would say this.' Manav asked and answering his own question he replied, 'She said that the IPL season is soon going to air, if you wish we can schedule our trip after that.'

'So?' We girls asked in unison.

'So?' He asked dramatically, 'That's massive man. And I know that girls like you will never understand'.

'Hey! What do you mean by that?' I asked.

As Manav shrugged and the girls made faces, I saw an opportunity and spoke. 'Never mind. Guys, I have to say something.'

'I am dating this guy, who also happens to be my boss and I really really like him.' I made my big announcement.

'Oh my god,' the girls shrieked in response. We three had a group hug. Manav was left alone.

'Well, I was expecting this kind of response from you lot and Nitya, you stole my limelight,' he said like the abandoned salad on a plate of hot pakoras.

'Fling with a boss? Brave you are. Show his picture,' Malvika said.

I was anxiously waiting for the girls' reaction when they see Rudra.

I showed a picture of him which I had secretly clicked during our morning meets. He looked like a Greek god. I wanted Komal, Malvika and Manav to like him. Yes, I needed my best friends' approval like my life depended on their feedback. I felt nervous.

Komal and Malvika gasped for a breath.

'No way,' Malvika shook her head. 'Is this guy for real? He looks like the one in Cadbury advertisements.'

'Mamma mia. He is like a celebrity but just into a wrong profession.' Komal let out a slow whistle. 'I don't believe that you are dating him.'

'Why?' I said looking in her eyes, 'You think that I am not worthy of a guy like him?'

'Ehh..' Komal was short of words. I opened my mouth in disbelief.

'Joking yaar,' Komal tried to me give me consolation, 'you both look sexy together…like Brad Pitt and Angelina Jolie'

'He's quite OK, I think. So-so types,' Manav waved his hand.

I looked at Malvika. She lip-synced the word 'jealous'.

'Have you seen Yogi?' Manav produced his cell phone. Unfortunately, he drew a poor reception from us.

Yogi was a pretty girl with chubby cheeks and shoulder length hair.

'Awww she is so pretty...' Komal said and quickly turned her attention towards Rudra's other photos.

'Leave it. I don't need your pity compliments.' Manav was upset.

'When do we get to meet the boss?' Malvika twitched her eyebrows.

'Soon, soon,' I said. It was high time that I take this relationship to the next stage.

'YES OR NO?' my mom threatened me the next morning. She had a ladle dipped in kadhi which she frequently raised as a weapon. *What has got into her.*

'Mom please…' I tried to reason with her, keeping a safe distance anyway.

'No. You tell me one thing. Yes or no,' mom cried a little louder this time. 'You want to arrange a second meeting with Jignesh or not?'

'Mom please.. I said naa... he is too Gujju for my taste.'

'*Tasteeee*?' She screamed and stretched the word 'taste' about ten times synchronously. 'You are talking about taste? This is not your fast food, understand? Too Gujju for my taste, huh. And what's wrong with Gujarati people? You are also one of them. You drink beer, you come home late...you will hang my head in shame one day.'

'You think your mom is stupid, you think that I don't know anything…you rejected him for that good for nothing Hitesh…I told you a hundred times then also,' she was uncontrollable. This was the millionth time she had said her 'I told you so' in Hitesh's case.

I had a strong feeling that Pappu uncle or Jaina maasi must have called her early in the morning or some other sluggish relative must have initiated this forest fire.

'Ok mom, just let me think. We will discuss this in the evening when I come from work,' I said grabbing my bag and running like the hit and run accused towards the door without looking back. I could see at least three neighbours eavesdropping, and pretending to talk amongst themselves as I banged the door shut.

'I will throw you out if you don't decide by evening. You are staying in my house, don't forget that.' Mom called after me. *Why do parents have to remind you that they have been providing you with shelter?* I had to talk to Rudra today...the typical, 'where is this relationship going'. I didn't give a damn if it made me look desperate or gave me a second heartbreak.

I paced outside his cabin restlessly without making it oblivious to other colleagues. He was not inside. That was so unlike him. He must have gotten late, but then again, he was never late. A couple of co-workers passed by, looking at me and then laughing secretly. I was confused.

'Looking for someone?' Pooja wished me morning extra chirpily. I don't know but her happiness made me suspicious like something bad is going to happen. 'Here, I brought coffee for you.'

'Yeah actually, I have some problem with the audit of Shivam Jewellers so I am waiting for Rudra sir.

'Rudra sir is out for a meeting,' Pooja replied coolly. Her face seemed to have a different kind of satisfaction, like slaying an old enemy or something.

'I guess I will come later then,' I said making way towards my desk. *Why was everyone staring at me? Was I looking that hot today? No wait. They were giving me strange expressions.*

'Have a nice day!' Pooja raised her coffee mug and smiled.

I switched on my computer. I had about thirteen emails to go through and one of them was from Rudra. The subject line 'Breach of order' made me curious. I had to open it first.

*Dear Nitya,*

*Yesterday you left the office without your manager's permission. Also I had assigned you a task to kiss me back which you left incomplete. Neither did you wait for your boss to give you a lift back home so that he could fulfil the unfinished. You have shown inadequacy in the project assigned to you. I hope you will be efficient in it after today's overtime. If you don't want to be sacked, then today this project should enter the completion mode.*

*Yours & always yours,*

*Rudra Desai,*

*Branch Manager, Axis Bank, Nanpura, Surat*

*PS: Warning – a kissing predator is at large.*

Some smiles bring out the stupid in you. Mine was one such smile. He had signed 'yours & only your'. He was mine, my property. Slowly my eyes reached to the recipients. Agarwal Pooja, Batra Rakesh, Bhimani Ajay… and so on. *Oh shit!* I nearly expired.

Rudra had sent this message to all by mistake. Crap. Even to the cluster head. My head started spinning wildly. My body temperature shot up. Now I understood why everyone around me was giving weird looks.

Pooja leaned on Jhanvi's desk and blew on her hot coffee, her eyes at me. I just sat there pretending to work while I absorbed the shock.

'Really hats off to her guts. She is still here,' Pooja told Jhanvi, loud enough so that I could hear.

'Shh…I am working,' Jhanvi said to fend off Pooja. Jhanvi had perhaps decided to stay neutral.

'But some people get paid for kissing their boss, right Ajay?' Pooja laughed solo. Ajay kept his eyes fixed on the computer screen without looking at me. He was saving me the embarrassment.

'There is a term for such cheap girls,' Pooja blurted.

'Enough.' I raised my palm at her.

'Jhanvi, I have to be at a client's office. I am leaving.'

'By the way, you know Jhanvi, Rudra sir is meeting a girl for marriage today,' Pooja passed this information to me indirectly. 'I saw him leaving the office with an extremely beautiful girl.'

'Such a douche, kissing one girl and marrying another,' she added.

Blood began to rush to my face and I could feel the heat. And the worst part was that I was not able to hide it. Pooja's information was never wrong, she couldn't have been lying.

She was delighting every micro-millisecond in my misery.

'Coffee Culture has some great pastries, little pricey but the taste is matchless.' Pooja made a one-way conversation with Jhanvi.

I stood still, unsure of what actions I should take next. My brain started to freeze. I squeezed the top of my nose with my eyes closed.

I nearly sprinted out of the office.

'Where madam?' an auto driver came front.

'Coffee Culture, Parle Point. Drive fast'

HE SAT THERE with a girl with two tall glasses of coffee topped with ice-cream. They were near the window and I could see through the glass that they were in a deep serious conversation. I felt like breaking the window. I know that we are not officially dating or something, but I can't see him giving someone else the attention which I always wanted from him. I felt like pulling the girl by her hair and dragging her out of the cafe.

*That person is mine. Don't even breathe around him.*

I stormed inside.

'Table for how many,' the waiter asked though the whole place was nearly empty. I ignored him and marched to Rudra's table.

The laughter of the girl was interrupted by my sudden arrival.

I gave her a cold shoulder while she looked at me confused, and bore my eyes straight into Rudra's eyes. I didn't care what explanation Rudra had to give for my behaviour.

'Hi,' he said, his expression calm. *How can he be so placid?* Anger built up in my eyes as I looked at him and that girl in succession. I kept looking into his eyes for five more seconds and then I turned to go.

'Wait,' he said tugging my hand. He pulled out his wallet to pay for the coffee.

I jerked my hand off from his hold, didn't look back and kept walking. I went to the first auto I saw.

'Not going madam,' an irate rickshaw driver said, who had just woken up from an afternoon nap.

'Ghoddod road,' I replied pushing back my tears.

'No, I am not going that way,' he denied.

'Then Rander road.'

'Too much traffic there. You take some other auto,' he said more interested in going back to sleep.

'I will pay you a hundred rupees,' I bribed. Rander road takes no more than forty rupees.

He signalled me to get into the auto. I saw Rudra crossing the road towards my auto. He was already halfway near the divider, waiting for the cars to pass by.

'*Jaldi bhai, jaldi chalavo.*'

He pulled the ignition rod and luckily it started in one go. Rudra was about one feet away when our auto left. I broke into tears. I was so proud that I had managed to control myself in front of him. I couldn't let him know that he had the capacity to control my emotions. The autowala kept looking in his rear view mirror to check if I was ok.

'*Lo ben, pani piyo,*' he handed me a plastic Pepsi bottle filled with water.

I accepted it gratefully.

Five minutes later, I called home.

'Mom…' I said trying to sound calm, 'arrange a second meeting with Jignesh'.

'That's what I am saying...he is a very good guy and family is also well settled,' her voice had an adrenaline rush. 'But where are you? You are not in office,' she asked hearing the sound of traffic in the background.

'I am going to meet a client, will be back in the evening. Speak later.' I switched off my phone.

'Rander road has started, where do you want to go?' the autowala asked, breaking the stream of my thoughts.

I wanted to go to a place where I could scream and cry out loudly like a maniac, without anyone asking me what had happened.

'Stop when you see a cyber café.'

I knew what I wanted.

I CAME TO office at six. Everyone had left early since the boss was not around. Only Ajay was there. My nose was still red from all the crying and my eyes were a little swollen.

'What happened? Where were you?' Ajay asked concerned. 'Even your mobile was switched off. Are you ok?'

'I am good. Is Rudra sir in his cabin?' I asked

'No. He left in the morning for the matrimonial meeting. He hasn't come after that.'

'Ok. Could you please give this to him tomorrow when he comes?' I handed him a sealed envelope.

'What is this?'

'My resignation letter.'

'What?' His mouth fell open. 'Why? But see, this is not a big issue...'

'I am getting married, so... I am planning to take a break from work,' I told him. I hoped that my message would be passed to Rudra loud and clear.

'Oh,' he said, his voice small. 'I mean great. Congratulations.'

AFTER JIGNESH AND his family left, I slumped on the couch and began to look outside the window.

'They are asking us to perform the gaud-dhana day after tomorrow only. How will we do all these arrangements at such a short notice?' My mom was worried about a ceremony which takes only one hour to wrap up.

I didn't say anything. I laid my head on one of the cushions and left my legs hanging on the other arm of the sofa.

'Let's call Girish kaka and Pappu uncle for the good news,' she said walking towards the phone.

She avoided talking to me and pretended that everything was fine or will be fine once I got married.

She was about to dial Pappu uncle's number when the cordless phone rang in her hand.

'Jai shri Krishna. Yes, I am Hema ben. *Aap kaun*?' she asked.

'Yes, yes, she is my daughter. Chartered Accountant,' she said. I looked up to her as to who could be asking for me.

'Today? Now? But we just fixed her alliance two hours back,' she replied. 'No, no, only second meeting. Gaud dhana is day after tomorrow. *Shubh divas chhe*.'

'What does your son do? What is his height?' she asked.

'Evening is fine. Yes, yes, we are at home only. Ok. Ok. Jai Shri Krishna.' She cut the line.

'Who was it?'

'Some Navin bhai from Mumbai. He is coming with his wife and son here in three hours.'

'I don't want to meet any more boys. Jignesh is fine.'

'Just see this last one. If you don't like, then gaud dhana is scheduled for day after tomorrow anyway. And see, you don't even have to change. You are already ready and we will serve them snacks in the same plates as Jignesh's,' she said.

'No, I have decided. I am the head of the family,' I said to lighten the mood.

'No problem, I am the neck. I can turn the head any way I want,' said my witty mom.

The doorbell rang at exactly five in the evening. Savita ben opened the door to three people. As the uncle of the group came in, I got a chance to look at his son. I stopped in my tracks.

It was Rudra Desai.

FOR A SECOND my heart stopped beating. My breathing was raised like an asthma patient.

'Rudra...sir...' I said when I gathered myself. He gave me a secretive smirk as his family settled on the sofa. He looked so handsome that he could make any girl weak in the knees.

*Surely he can't be here to ask for my hand. I must be dreaming or this must be a spoof.*

'You know him?' My mom asked me.

'You know her?' His mom asked him.

'Huh?' I was still in a state of shock, 'Yes he is my manager'. I tried to restrain the happiness flooding inside me. His parents seemed utterly surprised.

'Oh, I didn't know that you stay here,' Rudra acted surprised. 'I thought that this is some other Nitya Trivedi,' he lied so subtly.

'You work at her bank?' His mother asked him.

*If he is my manager then which bank is he going to work in, mummy ji?*

My mom signalled Savita ben to clear the table and bring new plates with snacks, while his mom casually scanned our living room.

'Good, good so you know each other,' his father said. Rudra was the subset of his parents. Father's eyes and mother's features.

'Where do you stay in Surat?' My mom asked.

'Originally we are from Mumbai. Rudra got a transfer here last year,' his father paused to sip some water. He wore a crisp white half sleeve shirt and an expensive watch. His glasses had gold rim and he looked like one of those uncles who could give you a complete vocational guidance after twelfth standard. 'So sometimes we come to Surat to see him and most of the times, he comes to Mumbai.'

My mom kept a constant nod. 'What do you do in Mumbai?'

'I am the head of chemistry department in Jamnadas College in Mumbai,' he said.

'I was also a teacher in a primary school. They were offering me the principal's post, but at that time my Nitya had to take her board exams, so I didn't accept... How to handle extra responsibilities with kids studying?' My mom said. Salute to parents who don't think twice before giving up their career for their children.

'True that. Even when my Rudra was taking his boards, we cancelled our cable connection and I was with him at home, only looking after him,' his mom narrated her saga.

There I was sitting opposite Rudra's parents. The hottest guy. I felt like complimenting his parents that I was a big fan of their work.

Silence. Everyone exchanged glances and kept smiling. I felt her mom's fleeting eyes on me. I became very conscious. *She is Rudra Desai's mom. Will she ask me to show her how I walk?*

'Where is your native?' Uncle finally broke the silence.

'We are originally from Surat only. My birth was here and so is Nitya's. Her father was from Ahmedabad,' my mother gave an insight into our origins.

'I am from Delhi but ours was a love marriage. He was transferred to Delhi and we met there,' his mother gave information about her descent. 'You have only one daughter? No son?'

'Yes, I have only one daughter. Does Rudra have any siblings?'

'Rudra has an elder sister Mitali. She is married in Hyderabad. She has a two-year-old son also. Our son-in-law is in the Air-force.'

*Aryan, his nephew. I remember.*

'Where do you stay in Mumbai? I have some relatives in Kandivali and Borivali,' my mom asked his father. A quarter of Gujarati population resides in the Borivali neighbourhood of Mumbai.

'In Powai.'

'Go beta go, speak to him in private. Although you know him, but for matrimony, it is a different matter,' my mom told me after they had had some refreshments. '*Thik hai na*?' she turned towards his parents.

'Absolutely. We are very forward-thinking people. Go Rudra. You people talk,' his mother told him.

My heart thumped as I led him to my bedroom.

'HI,' HE SAID calmly.

'Hi,' I replied in a tiny voice. I sat on one end of the bed assuming that he will sit on the other. He walked around in my room and chose to lean on the window instead. He wore my favourite black shirt paired with slim fit cream chinos. His hands were in his pockets. He looked a class apart, a little wary, but still class apart.

'I always wanted to see your room and how my car looked like from here. Is this the place where you used to call me from?' He asked peeking his head out, thrilled. Here lived Vodafone's most esteemed customer.

*Why was he reminding me?* I nodded, still not ready to make a conversation.

'You didn't pick up my phone yesterday?' He asked, his voice gentle.

'I didn't see any reason to.'

'Ahan.' Silence.

'And you handed your resignation letter?'

'Yes, my alliance is fixed,' I looked directly at him to be able to see his expression. I had practised countless times in my mind how I would break this news to him. I wanted to see his reaction. I wanted him to be hurt. In fact, I thought about how I would break this news to Rudra more than I thought about Jignesh.

'So? Giving up your job?'

'No way. If I am not working for you, doesn't mean I will not work at all.' I looked sharply in his direction. 'I might join my fiance's business. I have better opportunities.'

'To-be fiancé,' he corrected me. He looked dangerously angry.

More silence prevailed.

'And what about us? What about this…this bond that we share?' he asked.

'Bond? Ohhh!' I rolled my eyes. 'Which bond are you talking about? Does this bond have any name? Is it a government bond? Atomic Bond? Or a peptide bond? No wait, it should be James Bond,' I said. He gave a lopsided grin. However mad I was at him, I was still happy with the fact that I had the capability to make him smile.

'And what is it with your status update?' He fished out his iPhone and began to read aloud. 'Don't keep a girl waiting for too long. While you are busy making up your mind, she might change hers.'

He tried to suppress his laughter. 'Like seriously?'

'My status was not for you,' I said, 'but if the shoe fits then tie the lace and wear it'.

'The girl who I was having coffee with, was my cousin. My *foi's* daughter,' he explained. 'She was going to elope with this guy from her college and wanted me to sign as her witness. So I had to rush and explain to her to not to take this drastic step.'

My eyes and my mouth were opened with shock and embarrassment. I was the mother of overreaction. When negative things happen around you, you start seeing every person and situation in a negative context. Seriously, why do any women have to overthink and then over-react.

'But why did you act like that?' He asked gently.

'Pooja told me that a really beautiful woman came and you cancelled all the meetings to be with her. And I am one jealous woman. I can't bring myself to imagine you with other woman. Probably I know more about your exes than you do. I know that there was no oral commitment between us but seeing you with some other girl there made my insides burn with anger…' my voice trailed off.

'Before you assume, why don't you try this crazy method called asking? Wait, how do you know about my exes?' He was clearly underestimating a woman's research skills.

'That's not the point. The point is that after what happened with Hitesh I thought all guys are same.'

'If all guys are same then why do you women take a lot of time in choosing one?' He said playfully. He had a point.

'Don't you understand hints? Don't you know the secret admirer who kept flowers at your desk?' He asked. I thought it was Ajay.

'Why would I dare to ask you out though I knew that you were seeing guys for matrimony?' He said as he came close to me.

He held be by my shoulders and said, 'Nitya, can't you see it?'

My eyes became moist.

'I wanted you in my life since the day I set my eyes on you, unless you have forgotten that douche. What was his name? Hatim tai?'

I smiled.

'Some people stay in your mind longer than they stay in your life and that was a huge mistake and nothing more.'

'I am falling for you,' he said.

'But I thought that your taste in women is different…' I said.

Look at you, you are perfection.

'What do you think men like? Do you think I like Pooja? You think that I don't know what she is doing? Please give me some credit, I more than that.'

I paid attention.

'I see you every morning. You greet me with a smile while everyone else is scowling. I am nothing without that first cup of extra strong coffee which you make. That is enough to make my day.'

'Really? I never thought of it like that. It's just a habit.' I was astounded by his confession.

'Remember, that day when our peon Gopalbhai hurt his finger, you did his dressing so meticulously. This extra-ordinary caring thing makes you exotic.'

'You are eight hours on your desk and then you press your palms on the back of your neck and that drives me nuts.'

'Oh,' I said. Such intricate details.

'That rubber band pencil combo holding up your hair makes you sexy.'

'When you move about in the office, sometimes I can catch only a glimpse of you. Don't take me as a creep, but I fantasise about staring at you for one whole minute without any interruption.'

I looked up at his face. Such a candid confession.

'One day you are all in western formals and the next day you are a totally desi girl. You beguile me. So many moods you have. You look so innocent in the pink dupatta of yours. That's my favourite.'

There was genuineness ringing in his voice. He can't be lying. I smiled.

'I thought you would never agree for bike stunts. But you pleasantly proved me wrong. The girl who said no to everything, agreed to the most dangerous adventure. Makes me ask myself, who is this mysterious girl? I like this confidence.

'And I don't know, when and how, but amongst all these small things, I fell for you. You are a difficult girl. But then, difficult girls are worth it.'

I was so overwhelmed. I placed my hand on his mouth. My eyes brimmed as my hormones began to take over.

'Rudra, you showed me a side of me, which I didn't even know existed. You make me feel alive. Every day with you is a surprise. All these words of yours...' I shook my head. 'You have showed me my worth. When everyone expects you to change everything to get a suitable groom, you were the one who made me love myself. Now that I am all head over heels in love with you... I don't think I can imagine my life with anyone but you.' I gave a monologue.

He placed a palm on my cheek affectionately.

'Nitya Trivedi, you are everything to me and I will always love you...till the end of time.'

'I love you too. And I know that you are the one person I want to spend my whole life with.'

He looked into my eyes, his gaze intense. He came close to me, his eyes fixed on my lips. He took my face in his palms and gently kissed me. A million butterflies flew in my stomach.

The best feeling in the world is kissing someone for the first time when you have really wanted to kiss them for a long time.

After a few seconds, I pushed him away gently. *I can't do this. Not when our parents are policing us around.*

'Did you read the email? You know what those people were saying about it in the office?' I said. Pooja's words, 'there is a term for such cheap girls' haunted me.

'Screw that. The 'what will people say' question has killed more dreams than anything else in the world. I want you and that's all I know,' he said. 'I don't know how could I be so stupid. How could I make a mistake of sending that email to all? I have spoken to our cluster head. He thought that I was harassing you sexually.'

'What did you say?' I asked worried.

'I said that that was not the case. She is my to-be fiancée.'

'What?' My eyes widened with shock. 'No, you did not. What if I had denied?'

'I knew you wouldn't.'

'Over-confidence?'

'Very much.'

'Then what happened?'

'Nothing much. He issued a memo and warned me to keep my behaviour in check. But my job is saved.'

'I am sorry. It's my fault too.' I genuinely felt apologetic.

'Yes, it is. Had you kissed me on that day, I had no need to type that email,' he smiled. Playful Rudra was back again.

'Hmm and one more thing. Don't tell my mom that we already liked each other. She wants the credit of finding the suitable guy for me. Let her think that this is an arranged marriage.'

'Ok, so I will go out and say that I like the girl. Proceed for the gaud dhana ceremony.'

'But I might have to think. Perhaps arrange a second meeting,' I *bhao-khao-ed*.

He pulled my hair playfully. 'You want to think more, huh?'

'Wait. Have some patience. We have to at least act *naa* that this whole episode is arranged. My mom is very smart, mind you.'

He laughed. 'Why are you so scared of your mom?'

'Not scared. But I want her to have the satisfaction that she has accomplished her duty as a mother.'

'And like I said, I need more time to think.'

'Achha, you need more time even after kissing me?' He smiled as he turned the knob to open the door.

NEXT MORNING, WE went to Rudra's home for a second meeting. It was just a formality. They wanted Rudra's sister Mitali and Kshitij jijaji to come and meet us before taking any final decision. We had not ruled out Jignesh yet. Mom wanted to keep him as a buffer.

'After a year or so, I am planning to settle down in Mumbai itself,' he said. My mom listened carefully.

'What about you? After Nitya's marriage are you planning to stay in Surat only?' He asked taking a bite into the hotly-served Handvo by his mom. We Indians are very particular when it comes to serving food; we can't go cold turkey on that.

'Yes, why? Where else would I go?' My mom asked confused, maybe hoping he might invite her to join us in our honeymoon or something.

'I intend to stay with my parents after marriage in Mumbai, why don't you stay with us too? Or else you will be alone here with no one to look after you,' he said in a no-nonsense tone. This was a shocker. This guy cannot be for real. I could see that my mom was ready to do my gaud-dhana with him right there, even before he finished his sentence.

But maybe this did not go down too well with his mother as she choked on the Kaju barfi. I think she did not fancy seeing her daughter-in-law's mother stay too close to her.

'I mean, if you are not comfortable in staying together, at least you can rent a flat in the same building closer to Nitya,' he extinguished the fire-sparks as soon as he smelled danger.

They say that you don't get a second chance to make the first impression and my God, Rudra made sure that my mom did not have any reason to rule him out. This whole closer-to-Nitya thing was working. Which parents, which parents in the world would not want to stay close to their married daughter?

The more he spoke, the more I realized why it didn't work out with Hitesh.

'No, no, how I can stay with my daughter after her marriage?' My mom blushed. Of course she was relishing over the possibility of her actually coming to stay in Mumbai. 'I don't even have anybody there'.

'Why not? Nitya told me that you have a cousin in Mumbai,' Rudra said, on which my mom curled up her lip, eliciting the pain Jaina maasi had caused her. 'And it is even closer to Singapore, where Nitya's uncle lives. You can take a direct flight without having to travel in trains from Surat.'

I left like applauding for Rudra's pitch. In office, where he said that if you recognize what a client wants and see from his mind-set your half job is done, all of us yawned. Today when he was using his professional skills to lock in the client, I totally understood the importance of his gospel.

And for the first time in twenty-seven years of my life, I saw my mother speechless. Sometimes in today's age where parents are side-ruled by their children when it comes to choosing a partner for marriage, meeting a prospect who completely understands that there is a family involved and to be taken care of is rare to find.

'Wow, you have such long hair. Give me some tips to grow them,' his sister complimented me.

After that, she introduced me to her husband on Skype.

'Hema ben, we like your daughter,' his father said after he got a consenting nod from his wife. 'Now it is up to you and Nitya to decide.'

Mom looked at me. She already knew my answer.

'Rudra saw so many girls but kept rejecting everyone. What to do? These days young people marry late, have children late and then it will be too late.'

'This is what I keep telling my Nitya, But no. Arey Manika ben, we have seen so many guys for her. But she keeps finding little faults.'

'What do you say? Should we proceed?' My mom asked me in front of everyone. My cheeks turned beet-red. It's happening. It's real.

'Yes,' I nodded. *God this is embarrassing.*

'And Rudra? You are sure na?' His father asked him.

'Sure,' he said without looking at me. *He looks so cute when shy.*

'Hundred percent?' My mom pulled his leg.

'Arey hundred and ten per cent,' he said and everyone in the room burst into laughter.

SOON AFTER WE came home, the first thing my mom did was to call Jignesh's family and break off the deal.

'Out of all the boys we saw for you, this was the best,' my mom accepted as she sipped her afternoon tea as I was having my coffee.

'Hmm ...' I said.

'After all, who found the guy?'

'Who found?'

'Arey they saw the matrimonial advertisement I gave about you in *Gujarat Samachar* and then they contacted us. Rudra told me,' she wanted the credit.

'Of course this alliance is fixed only because of you.' I acknowledged her hard work, smiling inwardly.

'Who are you calling now?' I asked.

'Taking approval from everyone, what else?' She said. I got really tensed.

'Arey this is just a formality,' she said, 'guy is fixed only'.

Thank God! My senses calmed down.

MY WEDDING WAS attended by the farthest uncles and their plumpest kids whose faces I saw for the first time. Because I was one and only daughter, mom wanted to do a big fat wedding. No one should be left out. Not even sensitive relatives.

'Oh hi Jaina maasi. *Kem chho*? How is Pinky? She got settled in US?'

'Good, good. Pinky and Dollarkumar are also fine. Her visa came last month so she went there last week only. I packed *theplas* and pickles for her. You check, she has put up her pictures on Facelook.'

'You should have done a detailed background check of the groom's side.' Many touchy relatives gave their input to my mom. Apparently they were feeling bad because their opinion was not asked before fixing my alliance. Seriously you can't make everyone happy.

Pappu uncle called me in another room. He wanted to discuss something in private. 'See beta, if you are not happy with this wedding then just tell me. Don't hesitate. I will cancel all the arrangements.' He said this while eating my wedding *laddu*. Relatives asking offending questions is the societal norm. I wished he choke on the tiny almond pieces and shut up permanently.

'Thanks uncle for your concern. It means a lot,' I said, 'but the thing is that I couldn't be any happier.'

Today I am not going to allow him spoil my mood.

Another uncle who was in charge of the flower arrangements stopped me midway.

'Nitya beta, come here. Come here. You do service in Axis Bank, no? What is your salary? When did you get your appraisal?' Uncle asked me scary questions without realizing that I am embarrassed.

'Uncle I…' I hesitated.

'Your mom was telling that you earn fifty-five thousand per month. Talk to your bank no for Montu's job for a good post. He just completed his B.Com last year. Now you only will have to take care of your younger siblings no,' he said like I was in charge of issuing jobs.

'No problem uncle, just tell him to forward me his resume. I will forward it to the HR department.' I excused myself jotting down my email ID on a piece of paper.

'Khushbu also wants to do CA. What do you say? What is the scope?'Another uncle in the group asked me for his daughter.

I felt very important as everyone took my valuable advice for career counselling.

'Oh you were searching for a boy on computer? Teach us also this internet.' Another uncle guffawed. I excused myself to check into the group of aunties.

'Jamai vegetarian *hai na*?' One of the aunties asked my mom.

'Pure veg… pure veg… I strictly told my Nitya that don't bring any fisherman in this house,' my mom replied.

'But he is not brahman. He is an outcaste,' another aunty opposed. She firmly believed that no girl can get a complete package and there should be at least some compromise.

'He is not a brahman, but he does not have any bad habits, is a CA and looks like a hero. A-one. These days even some brahmans have started eating eggs and gone out of line,' mom referred to that aunty's daughter who was objecting. She kept quite.

'Come here,' my grandmother signaled me. '*Dimaag shaant chhe ne?*' Perhaps the only one to ask me the most sane and meaningful question.

I smiled. 'Yes Ba. Better than me.'

'Good. That's the main thing. What else do we want in life?'

'AWW...DI FINALLY YOU are getting married huh? Am so happy for you..' one of my younger cousins said since everyone had lost hopes that I will not be able to secure a guy, 'you finally did it'.

*I have not cracked the IAS entrance.*

'Be careful,' I said maintaining a safe distance so as to not ruin my mehendi. 'Thanks and now you are next in line. So finding a guy on your own or through the relative' way?'

'You only find for me... a handsome guy like Rudra jijaji... what a dashing personality... does he have any cousins?' Hemal said. She was Pappu uncle's daughter.

'Sorry there is only one piece like that. But Pappu uncle has so many contacts. Sure he will find a wonderful guy for you.' I smiled. 'Ok tell me what type of boy you want?'

'Oh please... not that type of guy you see in Indian serials. *Adarsh damad* (ideal son-in-law) kind of crap. I want someone who treats me his equal...'

'Rudra is very handsome yaar... total envy material,' Monali bhabhi hugged me.

'Thanks bhabhi,' I said trying to protect my wedding Mehendi by construct a protective wall of mehendi walis around me.

'Finally you too fell for arranged marriage huh? But I think that love marriage is still better,' Monali bhabhi vouched for a love marriage.

'Why is that?' I asked her.

'Because a known enemy is better than an unknown friend.' Everyone burst into tiny giggles.

'First six months are very lovey-dovey, all hearts and roses but after that reality will creep in,' Monali bhabhi said while I carved Rudra's name on my hand. Komal, Malvika and Manav came next. Everybody pulled my hand to have a glimpse of the bridal mehendi. Manav wrote the name Yogeshwari in his right hand with a spare mehedi cone.

'You have totally lost it,' I told him.

My mom's most awaited function Grahshanti pooja was held the next day. All the ladies sang religious songs in tune with the music of latest Bollywood song in the background.

That evening we hosted a garba night in the communal compound of my building. Manav made arrangements for some Falguni Pathak garba CDs and we danced away to Sanedo (for those who don't know it's the quintessential garba song, it's a rage).

While the aunties indulged in the simple traditional steps circling an imaginary focal point the youngsters did some more complicated moves as the beats grew faster. It's amazing how we as Indians will need an auto for a ten minute walkable distance but still will not be tired of four hours of non-stop garba. Rudra wore a blue colored sherwani co-ordinating with my lehenga. He was undoubtedly the most spectacular guy there. He could really dance, he got moves.

THE NEXT MORNING was the most important morning of my life. I prayed the God to thank him. Just thank him.

I wore a red and white panetar (sari) with gota border for my wedding. The beautician had done a wonderful makeup and made me look like a doll.

And then the *baraat* came amongst fireworks and I saw him. He looked like a king. All Rudra's friends and family were dancing on 'saajan ji ghar aaye'.

'Wow... he looks stunning' I overheard some of the girls in the background. I felt so lucky to have him in my life.

My mom circled a plate with a diya and did a tika on his forehead and while he was trying to save his nose. In a very calculative move, my mom pinched it. A *naak-khenchvanu* ceremony to denote that mother-in-law will always be smarter than her *jamai*.

Rudra first saw me during the *Jaimala* ceremony. He gave a slow smile and discreetly did a thumbs up. His friends raised him sky high making it difficult for me to put the garland around his neck. My relatives raised me even higher so that we were almost equals. And while we were up in the air, I pulled his hand in an off-guard moment, drew him near and managed to place the garland around his neck. We got jeers from the crowd.

The wedding hall had chairs in the rear seats for not so important relatives and sofas in the front rows for the members of the groom's side. It was unbelievable how some of my relatives placed a napkin on their chairs to secure seats and went to run errands. They failed to differentiate a wedding hall from a local bus.

'What are we waiting for?' I asked the Pandit who made that emerald ring for me. He was the same who wrote my *horrorscope.*

'I wait for right muhurat. Right muhurat is eight thirty six so marriage vidhi starts as eight thirty six. You before time,' he said. I rolled my eyes. Till then the cameraman told us to pose in weird ways.

'You are the most important person in my life Nitya and I promise to take care of you forever,' Rudra said while tying the mangalsutra around my neck.

Imagine if we had kissed after our marriage like the western wedding, all aunties would have fainted.

'made for each other', 'awesome couple', 'you look too good together', 'you two complement each other', 'the best couple' were some of the admiring words I received.

'Sexy people...even Saif and Kareena couple is a runner up in front of you guys' Malvika said when we were on the stage.

Married ladies whispered '*sada suhagan raho*' in my ears one by one.

It was Monali bhabhi's turn next. '*Sada suhaagan raho* and tell me everything about your first night.'

'Never,' I said.

All our colleagues attended the wedding.

'Oh hi Pooja!' I smiled extra sweetly at her when she was on stage to congratulate me. She tried to fake a smile, 'You have met my husband Rudra, right?' I smiled more.

'Of course, of course. Congratulations and no hard feelings huh,' she said, desperate to make amends as Rudra was still her boss.

'*Kyaa jabarjast khaana tha...aahaa haa,*' I heard one of his folks praising the wedding dinner. Apparently the success of an Indian wedding is directly proportional to the number of people approving the food. Basically, all is well when the food goes down too well.

Then my relatives queued to feed me and Rudra. It was a dangerous for both of us because all our relatives were expressing their love in the terms of amount of food they made us eat.

During the vidaai ceremony, one of my aunts went overboard and cried more than my mother. She cried like someone died and I was not even that attached to her.

'Mom don't worry about anything. I will always be there,' I said tearfully.

'Take care and make me proud at your in-laws,' she said dabbing handkerchief on her eyes.

Pappu uncle and Girish uncle shook hands with Rudra and we sat in his range rover decorated with roses.

'IT'S UNPOSSIBLE. HOW could you lose in all three rounds?' his foi asked him when we were playing find the ring in the milk pot.

*Unpossible?*

I had a doubt that Rudra let me win all the three games to cheer me up.

Thankfully we booked a room in Holiday Inn for our first night so I had no females pushing me to his bedroom. Saved me the embarrassment.

'Nitya you look so beautiful today,' Rudra said as I began to remove my jewellery.

I blushed.

'Come here,' he said gently pulling my hands towards him 'I am so happy today and I am so lucky to have you in my life.'

'I have got more than I deserved,' I said emotionally.

'That's not true. We are equals,' he said and kissing my knuckles, one at a time. And then he saw me in my eyes.

'Enough talking. Let's make the most of this five star room,' he said switching off the lights.

'EVERYTHING IS OK no?' one of the Rudra's raunchy aunties asked me referring to my first wedding night experience in front of all other aunties when I went into my mother-in-law's room the next morning to return her the valuables so that she keeps them safe.

My face turned pink. I gave her a very embarrassed smile while keeping my eyes downcast.

'Now you have turned into a woman.' That aunty went on. I felt like placing my palms on my ears.

'Aunty, can you please give me that gold set for to wear for the evening.' I politely asked Rudra's mom.

'Aunty *nai beta*, call me mummy,' she said.

'Now Manika you rest, you daughter-in-law will handle all your responsibilities, isn't it?' Aunty went on and on 'Now you are in your *saasra*. So less fickleness and more maturity.'

Would it be rude if I ask her a manual of dos and don'ts in saasra and read on later?

'No no my daughter-in-law is very nice. And if she doesn't know anything then I am here no. I will make her efficient in everything.' Rudra's mom looked at me lovingly.

After completing the *Satyanarayan Katha*, me and Rudra sat on the sofa amidst all the relatives.

'Now when do we bring toys?' One of the older aunts told us.

I actually understood what she said but I acted dumb.

'*Arey* now bring a small one to play with,' she said and everyone started laughing.

My hands scratched for a head palm but I maintained the decorum.

'Small one is on the way,' Rudra announced. Everybody stopped laughing.

Rudra burst laughing. The joke was on them. Everyone took a deep breath.

'By the way you have brought your passport no?' He asked me quietly.

'Yeah why?' I asked.

'We are going Switzerland. And there is skydiving, bungee jumping and rafting on the bucket list,' he smiled.

I opened my mouth to say something but he squeezed my hand. If this was the bucket, then this trip was definitely on the brim.

'I don't know what to say.'

'Say thank you.' He smiled and we went back to greeting aunties.